SUPERHERO ME!

MORTALITY BITES SERIES

RAMY VANCE

KEEP EVOLVING STUDIOS

To Bunny Banshee - you changed everything.

SUPERHERO ME!

PART I
A BEGINNING OF SORTS

After a millennium of stalking his prey, there is one disease he is quite immune to: eagerness.

So he lurks in the shadows, watching her from a distance. She is with her friends, running in the snow, chasing after ghouls out of some false sense of responsibility.

This desire to do what she perceives as right, as good, will be her undoing. Her pursuit of good will exhaust her, drain her, eventually deplete her of who she is until there is nothing left.

That is when he will strike.

Still, that might take years, and he is no longer immortal. There is a bit of eagerness in him, and he decides to dip his hand into the chaos of Katrina Darling's life to hasten her exhaustion.

And when he sees the anomaly flying in the sky, he knows exactly what he must do …

1

DEMONS OF THE DESERT AND SUPERHEROES OF THE NORTH

ATE LAST NIGHT—

"What the—?" I growled as a giant scimitar swung over my head. Luckily for me, I'm short and I bent down just enough that the curved blade flew over me.

My head stayed attached to my neck. Sadly, a half-inch of my hair didn't.

"Hey," I shouted as strands of auburn hair cascaded around my face, "I just got a haircut!"

The creature stared down at me with glowing red eyes. Then he kicked me in the chin—hard. I went down, my knee crunching deep into the unpacked snow. I came to my senses pretty quick, raising my dirk in a defensive position as I anticipated another swing of his scimitar.

But no swing came. Instead the damn ghoul took off, running up the mountain and deeper into the forest.

"Come on, girl," a voice yelled in a Ghanaian accent. I could tell he was smiling despite the life and death situation because, of course, Egya always smiled. As in, never stopped. It was annoying.

"I'm coming. I'm coming," I shouted back—not smiling. "Be careful, these ghouls are seasoned."

It was a misconception that ghouls were mindless monsters. They were more like pack hunters with thousands of years of preternaturally honed instincts and experience wrapped into freakishly strong bodies.

"So am I," Egya said, brandishing his Ngombe—a blade that looked like a sword with a crescent moon at its top (if that crescent moon was as sharp as a scalpel and designed not only to kill your enemy, but to absolutely decimate him).

Egya would have been terrifying if he wasn't dressed in a bulky, goose-down North Face jacket, a thick red toque with a maple leaf on it and matching mittens. OK, he was still terrifying with a sword like that in his hands.

Hell, Tickle Me Elmo would be terrifying with that sword in his hands.

I tried to get to my feet, but before I could, powerful hands lifted me up. "Are you hurt, milady?" Deirdre asked.

I shook my head. "I'm fine," I said to my changeling roommate who stared at me with deeply concerned eyes.

Deirdre stabbed her broadsword into the snow and left it standing as she helped me to my feet. Upright, the sword was taller than me. She wore a tank top and a pair of tights, pink running shoes and nothing else, and I marveled at this gorgeous creature who was almost totally immune to the cold.

"Thank you. I'm fine. Really," I said, pulling off my cherub mask. I had gotten some snow under it and my cheeks were beginning to chill.

She nodded and picked up her broadsword. Staring up the hill where the ghoul had fled, Deirdre growled. "Good to hear, but that ghoul will still pay dearly for his transgressions against my—"

"We're on a capture mission—not kill," I said. Deirdre didn't look my way, her ire still directed up the mountain. I grabbed the changeling warrior's face and repeated, "Capture mission. No killing … got it?"

Telling a changeling warrior not to kill was akin to asking the Terminator to chill out and have a beer. It just wasn't in their nature. But Deirdre had sworn her sword arm to me—an oath the fae take very seriously.

She begrudgingly nodded, and the three of us made our way up the mountain.

↔

The ghouls had been spotted at the Mount Royal Cemetery digging up some graves. As far as culturally appropriate behavior goes, that was a big no-no. Not that they'd gotten the memo.

Since the gods left four years ago and expelled their denizens onto Earth, mythical creatures like ghouls, changelings, dragons, wendigos, kirins—and just about any other creature you once thought of as *not real*—have had to figure out how to live by human rules.

But human rules can be confusing, and *not digging up the dead and eating them* wasn't culturally inappropriate for a ghoul. Hence why this was a capture-only mission. Well, more like a humanitarian mission; we needed to explain to these creatures that what they were doing was disturbing the metaphorical villagers.

That was the plan, at least. But the plan had one hitch: we had to get them to listen.

It doesn't matter … we have to try, I thought.

"What doesn't matter?" Deirdre asked.

"Deirdre," Egya cackled, "don't mind her musings. She's just 'thinking on the outside' again."

It was true. I did have a nasty habit of airing my thoughts. And the more inappropriate they were, the louder they aired.

"Ahh, I see," Deirdre said, knowing my quirk well. She bent down, gesturing for us to stop. The tracks led up the mountain, which was strange; ghouls liked graveyards and tended to live there. It was their equivalent of living in a grocery store. But these creatures were running *away* from the cemetery. But then again, it also made sense they were trying to put as much distance between us and their home: they didn't know that we'd already scoped them out and knew all about their families living in the tombs of Mount Royal Cemetery. They were running away from the cemetery because they were trying to protect their families from ... well ... us.

Deirdre gestured for us to come to her side. She put a finger over her lips, asking us to be silent, and pointed up. That's when I saw what she was looking at. The tracks led farther up the hill, but the ghouls weren't there. Either they had doubled back or burned a bit of time to create false tracks, but they weren't there.

They were up a tree.

Without warning a—what do you call a group of ghouls? A gang? A gouging? Ahh, got it—a funeral of ghouls dropped from the trees, surrounding us.

There were six of them, all brandishing scimitars typical of their Arabian heritage.

Egya, Deirdre and I stood back-to-back, readying ourselves for battle.

"Still a capture-only mission?" Deirdre asked.

"Yes," I said, holding my dirk in a defensive position. "We can do this." Then calling out to the ghouls, I said, "We're not here to hurt you. But you guys can't keep doing what you're doing. Listen, there are facilities that can help you. Places where Others like yourselves can go to learn how to be mortal. Put down your—"

But before I could finish my sentence, we heard someone cry out, "When criminals in this world appear, and break the laws that they should fear, and frighten all who see or hear, the cry goes up both far and near ..."

"Underdog?" I said, staring up as the human-looking boy lowered from the sky in his red leotard and fluttering cape. The letter 'U' was monogrammed onto his chest. He also wore a black mask that was more the Dread Pirate Roberts than Underdog.

"Actually," the boy said, "I was going to go for Underboy or Underman, but neither quite worked. And since Underdog is already taken, I'm Under*dawg*, as in d-a-w-g." He emphasized the "awg" part of his secret identity.

"Not really much of a difference," I pointed out.

"Oh, it is. One is an actual dog."

"Cartoon dog," I added.

"But I'm a 'dawg.' As in down with the peeps, hip and human. In other words, I'm cool." His hands folded into the *hang loose* gesture.

"I'm not sure you know what cool is—"

But before I could finish, he whooshed down faster than an archangel and ... well, tried to save the day.

↔

Underdawg yelled, "Speed of lightning, roar of thunder!" and showing off that "speed of lightning," flew in a circle and tackled all six of the ghouls.

Although he was lightning fast, I couldn't help but note that he didn't fly in a straight line. And I didn't think that was on purpose: it was almost as if he *couldn't* fly in a straight line.

Straight line or not, he was fast, and the six ghouls didn't know what hit them as he cartoonishly wrapped them in row after row of rope.

Once he tied them up, he started pulling them up into the sky while singing, "Fighting all who rob or plunder ... Underdawg. Underdawg!"

"What the—?" I said. "You're not going to hurt them, are you?"

"Ma'am," he said with a little airborne salute, "they are fiends of the night. I will dispose of them as is worthy of their ilk. By the way, totally dig the mask."

"Thank you, but not an answer. What are you going to do with them?"

"I was thinking about dropping them in the St. Lawrence River."

"And what? Drown them?"

He gave me a slurred, "Sure, why not?"

Why not? I thought with indignant fury. *Not. A. Good. Answer.* I threw my dirk, and luckily for the ghouls, my aim was true. My blade sliced the rope and they dropped into a nearby snowbank.

"Hey!" Underdawg cried out.

"Hey nothing. You're a red-underwear-wearing, poor excuse for a hero," Egya said. Good—the Ghanaian was distracting him.

"Deirdre!" I yelled. "Free them."

The changeling warrior moved forward without question, cutting their bonds.

"Scatter," I yelled. The ghouls didn't need to be told twice, and as they ran away, I cried out, "And no more grave-robbing!" Then I pointed up at Underdawg. "As for you. Superheroes don't drown anyone, let alone Others just trying to make their way on this Earth."

"Whatever," Underdawg said with a shrug. "I was just going for a test flight anyway." And before I could say anything, he flew up, up and away.

2

SUPERHEROES AREN'T REAL

"*S*uperheroes aren't real," I said.

"Are you sure?" my boyfriend Justin asked, kissing me on my forehead. He pulled me in close, our naked bodies joined in post-coital entanglement. (So much for taking it slow, then again, we've been dating for three months and he has lips to die for, so ...) This was my favorite part, because after three hundred years of having nasty, just-for-kicks vampire sex that usually ended with me eating the person, it felt great to cuddle.

Amazing, actually.

"I am sure," I hummed. "Very sure."

"How?" he said, sitting up slightly so he could look at me better. "How can you be so sure?"

"For one thing, I've been around a long, long time. For another, I'm not crazy. Superheroes don't exist."

"Sure they don't exist, but then again, neither did Others five years ago. And now the world is filled with all kinds of creatures I once thought were just in fairy tales. So if they're here, why can't super-heroes be here, too?"

"Fair enough," I said. "But still ..."

"Also, are you sure he wasn't just an Other burning some time to look like a super-strong boy who could fly?"

"I suppose. But the amount of power he displayed …" I trailed off, considering the implications. Every mythical creature had magical powers, but after the gods left, those powers were directly tied to their age. In other words, cast a fireball and you'd lose an hour or two of life. Fly like that … that would cost days—if not weeks—of time. "If Underdawg is an Other, he was burning through a hell of lot of time for nothing. And for what? A few ghouls in a forest? It just doesn't make sense."

"Maybe, but you've told me before that so many Others are lost. Maybe this particular Other is looking to go out with a bit of a bang. Save some lives, do some good, check out with his account well in the black."

Sitting up, I stared into Justin's impossibly beautiful eyes and raising a curious eyebrow at the expression, said, "Check out?"

"Yeah, check out. It's an expression for … you know, dying."

"I know. From the 1990s. I was around then, you know. I helped a lot of people 'check out,' and—" I stopped talking. I had meant that as fun banter, but there's nothing fun about all the lives I ended when I was a vampire. Nothing.

Justin must have sensed my change, because he shuffled down in the bed so we were face to face and gave me a hard kiss. "Balancing the account," he said. "That's what you're doing now. You're making up for all the wrong you've done."

"I can never make up for it all."

"No, you can't," he said. "But trying even though you know you'll fail is the best thing you can do. Heck, it's the best any of us can do. Which, if you carry that logic to its inevitable conclusion, means that you are the best of the best and—"

I kissed him. Hard. "Are you sure you're only nineteen?"

"Twenty in two months," he said.

"Well, I'm way more than twenty, and sometimes I absolutely marvel at your wisdom."

He giggled and placed a hand over his heart. "Old soul."

"Very old soul, indeed," I agreed, and gave him a kiss he'd remember (and by kiss, I mean more than a kiss. But I'm a lady, and ladies don't ... ahem ... kiss and tell).

↔

Once that was done, we fell into our cuddling position again, his arms around mine, silently breathing. Just when I thought he had drifted off to sleep, he whispered, "I wish I was a superhero."

"Why?" I asked, pulling his arm tighter around me.

"So I could go on missions with you guys."

It was a sore point for him that we wouldn't let him come along when we were trying to deal with some rogue Other or fix some misunderstanding between species. But it was for a good reason: I had three hundred years of experience as a vampire and a huntress. Egya was an ex-were-hyena, which meant he was annoying, and always had some stupid joke in the chamber, but he was also an incredible tracker and warrior.

And as for Deirdre, well, Deirdre was a changeling warrior. In the fae world, she'd be the equivalent of an elite warrior. Think Navy Seal, Marine, Ranger and MMA fighter all rolled into one, and you still wouldn't be close.

I touched my chest. "You're here. I carry you in my heart."

"Oh, ha ha. How very cheesy of you. But seriously, if I was a super-hero, I'd be by your side. Doing good, righting wrongs. Battling the forces of Mordor on campus."

"Hmph. Righting wrongs and fighting the forces of Mordor, eh? And tell me, superhero ... what would your superpowers be?"

"I don't know. Invisibility, for one. And the ability to turn kinetic energy into a blast ..."

"Like Black Panther."

"Black Panther and Harry Dresden's rings."

I nodded in approval. My super-hot boyfriend was a super geek, too. Definitely lucked out with this one. "Great. And your name would be ...?"

"Kinetic Man."

I turned around to face him. "Kinetic Man." I giggled. "That's a terrible superhero name."

"Good terrible?" he asked.

"Terrible, terrible."

"Still—"

My dorm room opened wide as Deirdre walked in, her barely clothed body covered in snow. "Sorry, milady," she said. "I saw the forewarning sock-on-door and knew not to enter, but there is something that requires your attention."

"What?" I said, sitting up and pulling the bed sheet to cover my more precious bits and bobs.

"Seems that Underdawg is in the halls of our residence."

"Here? Why?" I thought about all the Others living in Gardner Hall. There were a hell of a lot of people he might try to drop into a river.

"Excellent question. Underdawg is rather inebriated, and understanding his slurred speech is quite difficult. But from what I've gathered, he claims to live here."

3

DRUNKEN UNDERDOGS, DORM ROOMS AND SUSPICIOUS CHARACTERS

*D*eirdre led us to Gardner Hall's fifth floor, where we found a very drunk, very incoherent kid dressed up as Underdog banging on the bathroom door, crying, "Let me in!"

There were several kids standing around giggling at Underdawg, taking pictures and generally being unhelpful. So much for university camaraderie.

Then again, given how he was dressed, I didn't blame them for not … ahh … engaging.

I, on the other hand, was already desensitized to a boy dressed like a 1970's cartoon. "Hey kid," I said, walking up to him, "what's the problem? It's unlocked." I was wary of getting too close. After all, he was super strong and it was only by the grace of the GoneGods he hadn't smashed through the wall.

"I want to get into my room, but they won't let me in."

"Kid, I don't know where you think you are, but you're banging on the bathroom door. And again, it's unlocked."

He took a step back, peered at the universal symbol for a bathroom—which, being co-ed, had both a little man and woman on it—and shook his head. "That's not my room."

"That's what I was trying to tell you. Where's your room?" I got close and could smell cigarettes and the sweet, skunk-like smell of something a little more potent than tobacco. Made sense this kid liked the wacky tobacky. I imagine the cartoon *Underdog* is a lot of fun when you're high.

Underdawg looked around and shook his head as he thought about it.

"Do you know where your room is?" Justin asked, stepping forward.

I put a hand out, cautioning him not to get any closer. This clearly annoyed him, because he pushed past me and put a hand on Underdawg's shoulder. "Hey," he said, "do you know where you are?"

"I'm …" Underdawg started, but his voice trailed off.

"He's on the fourth floor," said a voice behind us. I turned to see a girl standing in her comfy flannel pajamas and, despite a fair amount of confidence I was only attracted to men, my jaw dropped.

To say she was beautiful would be akin to claiming that Adele is OK at singing. Words just don't do them justice. She was more than beautiful, even standing in probably the ugliest pajamas possible. I found myself swimming in her pristine eyes. And that was what made her truly unique: her eyes didn't match. One eye was ocean blue, and the other was mercury silver. Her hair was a rainbow of silver that cascaded down to the small of her back, each strand a slightly different shade of gray. And as for that smile … ships have been lost at sea looking for that smile.

And it wasn't just me; Justin had stopped moving, too. So had Deirdre, who simply muttered to herself in Elvish. I couldn't make out exactly what she was saying (my Elvish is rusty), but it was something along the lines of giving up her left thumb for a night with the silver-haired goddess. Then again, she might not have been saying "thumb" …

"Sorry," I said after a long moment of gawking.

"That's Bogdan—Boggie for short. He lives on my floor." She held up four fingers. "Fourth floor. Come on, Boggie." She held out a hand.

Boggie smiled when he saw the goddess. "Hi, Cassy," he said with an uncoordinated wave of his hand.

. . .

↔

I sent Justin back downstairs with Deirdre before his tongue tripped over his ... well ... tripped him up. Given how gorgeous and obviously turned on Deirdre was, I wasn't sure that was my best move. But hormones be damned—I needed a few answers, and those two weren't helping.

Cassy and I helped Underdawg back to his room, and given how he was moving, I could tell he wasn't very strong. Not at the moment, at least. He was too malleable, too easy to manipulate. Drunken creatures with immense strength often forget themselves and break walls with a careless toss of the arm. Or split a pool table into two by accident (a long story from my vampire days).

But this guy, he was flailing and falling and nothing was breaking. Hell, I was able to hold his arm down with barely any effort. It just didn't make sense after he'd taken down six ghouls by himself. Ghouls were Arnold Schwarzenegger strong—and I mean the Terminator, not Mr. Universe Arnie.

Whatever gave him strength has worn off. Or maybe it was an illusion, I thought.

"What gave him strength?" Cassy asked.

GoneGodDamn it! I was thinking out loud again. It was a nasty quirk I'd inherited from my vampire days. All that skulking around in an empty, dark castle got lonely, and talking to myself was one way to pass the time.

"Underdog would take that pill and become super strong," I said.

"But this guy is jelly. His strength must have worn off. Or maybe Underdawg was never strong, and it was just an illusion." I gave Cassy a shrug.

She lifted one gorgeous eyebrow. "You're the girl from the basement, aren't you?"

"Ahh, yeah?"

"Heard about you. You talk to yourself—a lot." We helped Boggie stumble down the hall toward his room.

"Glad to see my reputation precedes me."

"Oh, it does," she said with a playful wink that I'm pretty sure was what distracted the Titanic just before it hit that iceberg. "Here we are."

"Where?" I asked. Arrgh—me Titanic, my question the conversational iceberg!

She giggled. "Boggie's room."

"Ahh, yes. Of course. Do you have a key, or—"

"I'm HOME!" screamed Boggie. "I'm home, home, home!" He tried to do a little celebratory dance but wound up on his ass.

"Hey," someone yelled. A head popped out of the room four doors down. "Can we keep it down?"

"Sorry Harold," Cassy said.

"Sure you are," Harold said, slamming his door and making just as much noise as Boggie.

A couple more heads popped out, and one of them approached us. A large boy with black nail polish and long, blond hair. He also wore a dog's collar, which made him look like he belonged in some S&M club instead of a dorm. "Hey Cassy," he said, "need help?"

I could feel Cassy's body tighten as the goth kid approached. When he put a hand on her shoulder, she recoiled. She clearly did not like this kid.

"Thanks," I said, stepping between them, "but we've got it. We just need to fish through his, ahh, costume and find his keys."

The goth kid ran his painted fingernails through his hair while shaking his head. "Nah, I can get you in," he said. He fished out a quarter from his pocket and started jimmying the screw just above the keyhole. A couple of twists and he opened the door.

So much for dorm security.

"Voila." He made a little bow and smiled as he held the door open for us.

↔

Once inside, Cassy offered a curt "Thank you," and closed the door.

"Boy oh boy, you really don't like him," I whispered, just in case he was listening at the door.

"He's going to ..." Cassy started, but whatever she said after that was lost under the sound of Boggie diving gleefully onto his bed.

Cassy looked at me as if waiting for me to react to—what? Boggie's dive? I wasn't sure, but when I clearly didn't give her the reaction she was looking for, she sighed.

More than sighed. She looked as if I had hurt her feelings or offended her in some way. Way too sensitive, if you asked me. I thought about the goth kid outside and figured she was probably largely at fault for whatever reason she had for not liking him.

"So," I said, breaking the silence as Underdawg fell asleep, light drunken snores issuing from behind his mask, "we should probably roll him on his side just in case he pukes in the night. Maybe get a garbage pail, too."

Covering her gray eye, Cassy looked at Boggie through her ocean blue eye for a couple seconds before shaking her head. "No need. I'll be here." She went over to Boggie's desk and turned on his laptop. "I have some Netflix to catch up on, anyway."

Then she went very cold, giving me the unmistakable hint that it was time for me to leave.

Even when she was ignoring me, it was hard to stop staring at Cassy. *There's something about her...* I thought.

I shook my head to clear it—this was how impossibly beautiful people rendered the rest of us dumb and speechless—and, before things got awkward, I walked out into the now empty hall and down to my room in the basement.

4

A QUICK DISCUSSION AND A QUICKER OFFER DENIED

*D*ownstairs, Justin stood outside my room nervously biting his fingernails.

"What's going on?"

Justin turned beet red. "Look, I've only got eyes for you, but that girl was gorgeous, and Deirdre is now naked in your room. There's only so much my libido can take ..."

Arrgh—changeling roommate naked again.

"Deirdre," I said through the door, "what did we say about getting naked in front of people?"

"Not to do it, milady," a voice called from within my room.

"And about getting naked in front of my boyfriend?"

"Especially not to do it, milady," Deirdre called out.

"So why are you naked?"

"I'm not," she said as she opened our door and stepped into the hall. She wore creeper vines that cascaded down her neck. They covered her ... ahh ... pretty parts, but only from certain angles. A giggle or a quick turn would expose them in all their glory—which for a changeling was quite a bit of glory. "Is this not enough?"

"Not by a long shot," I said, grabbing her arm and taking her inside the room.

. . .

↔

As punishment for the little vine outfit, I made her put on my cotton bathrobe, which given our size difference stretched tight on her and did little to de-beautify her. Still, it would have to do. I called for Justin to come in, which he did, crawling into my bed and sighing deeply and loudly.

"I think we'd best try and get some sleep," I said.

"Good idea," Justin said, his voice lacking confidence in both my idea and his ability to ever fall asleep again.

"Yes, milady," Deirdre said, but instead of getting into bed, she stared at me. "One thought, though."

"Deirdre, can it wait until morning?" I asked. The trouble with changelings and "one thoughts" ... they usually involved going for an outdoor frolic.

Deirdre didn't move, but instead started blinking rapidly. I'd seen this behavior before—it was the fae's way of begging, which meant she was *beseeching me* to hear her one thought. This could go on for a while.

"OK," I said, "but I'm not leaving this room."

She groaned. "Very well, milady. Then one question."

"Fine. One question, but only one. Promise?"

Deirdre nodded. "The silver-haired goddess ..."

"Cassy?"

"Yes. Is she human?"

I narrowed my eyes. She looked human to me. An unreasonably beautiful human, but human nonetheless. But looks can be deceiving, and many Others' appearances only bore minor differences from humans. Deirdre was case in point: cover her pointy ears and you'd think she was a large, athletic, very pretty human.

Still, there were other things that made humans *human* and Others

Other. For one thing, mannerisms. Deirdre's rapid blinking would be a good example. No human does that.

Cassy was a bit off-putting, but in a very human way. Nothing about what she said or did spoke differently.

"Yes," I said. "I think so."

Justin shrugged. "Yeah, I agree. She definitely gave me a human vibe. Same vibe I'd get from Keira Knightley, or—"

"Hey, what happened to 'eyes only for me?' "

"Katrina Darling," he said. "Same vibe I get from Katrina Darling."

"Better."

Deirdre, who was clearly unimpressed by our cute banter, shook her head. "I am fae. We are a people accustomed to beauty. And yet I would have given my left nipple to be with her."

Ahh, I knew she didn't say thumb.

"Thumb?" Justin said.

Deirdre laughed. "Oh milady, you are very funny indeed." Then she turned to Justin. "In Elvish, nipple and thumb sound alike—"

"Deirdre, focus," I said.

"Of course, milady," she said, immediately cutting off her own thought. "It is just that we as a people do not succumb to beauty unless we are compelled to."

"And Cassy compelled you?"

The changeling shrugged. "It is possible."

"So what kind of Other could she be?"

"There is no Other who looks like her, no legend of silver hair that I know of, no myth involving undeniable beauty—save one."

"Sirens," I said, thinking back to what I knew about the creatures.

Deirdre nodded. "But the sirens drowned when the gods left, unable to leave their stone for safety."

I thought of the myth. Originally, sirens had been both male and female (although male historians tended to leave out the guys) who had wings or fish-like bodies. They would sit on rocks and draw in hapless sailors with their song, marooning them and ultimately killing them. But there were only eight known sirens, and when the gods left, none of the eight ever surfaced.

It was said that a fortnight after the gods left, the eight sirens got together and sang their songs to the heavens in an effort to lure the gods back. But the sirens were fated to die should their song not be heeded, so when the gods did not return, they flung themselves into the sea and drowned.

But that was the legend. There were no bodies found, no witnesses who'd seen the sirens actually die. For all we knew, they simply disbanded and were somewhere in the GoneGod World, trying to make their way as mortals.

And now my changeling roommate thought one of them was living in Gardner Hall, attending McGill University.

May the wonders never cease, I thought (in my head).

"OK," I said, "I'll do some research and see if any of the sirens' names were Cassy or if any of them were known for their silver hair. OK?"

Deirdre nodded, still standing. "One more thought."

"I said only one."

"Indeed, milady, but my original thought had an outdoor component to it. My revised thought is the same one in essence, but I have simply removed the need to go outside."

I sighed. "OK, what is it?"

"I disturbed your 'sock on the door.' "

"You did," I said. I didn't like where this was going.

"This Cassy has stirred old memories of when the fae would celebrate in the UnSeelie Court."

"And ... ?" I really, really didn't like where this was going. Justin sat up.

"Such celebrations were not only the duty of a changeling warrior, but also their pleasure. Perhaps I can make amends for disturbing you by helping to facilitate your love-making. I am proficient in ninety-three—"

"No," I said.

"No," Justin groaned.

"Very well, milady. But should you change your mind, you need only but ask." She removed my robe, revealing what Justin and I would be missing, before getting into her own bed.

5

A LEAGUE OF HEROES, RESEARCH AND MORE AWKWARDNESS

*T*he next day Justin woke me up with a kiss as he got ready for his early morning run. *Damn morning people*, I thought, and looking over at Deirdre's bed, I saw that she was already gone, too. Probably got up in the middle of the night to go sleep outside under the pines out back. She did that a lot.

I, on the other hand, didn't have class until 1pm and considered sleeping until then. *Duty calls*, I groaned to myself as I hauled my butt out of bed. I needed to figure out who Underdawg was and investigate if Deirdre's concerns about Cassy held any merit. Which meant—oh yay—studying. As if I didn't have enough research with my normal class load.

I got dressed in a nice little number I picked out—a cute Madeleine top with a high collar and a pair of cropped leather trousers—and completely ruined the outfit by covering it up with my snow pants and a ridiculously baggy (but warm) North Face jacket. I swear to the GoneGods, I don't know why I even try in winter.

Dressed, I made my way upstairs. On the windows were several posters, all the usual stuff: ads for tutors, flyers for an exhibit of cursed items at the Museum of Fine Arts, promos for various student-friendly bars and restaurants and … what the hell? Taped to the window were several posters of the kid—Harold, was it?—who'd leaned out his door to yell at me when I was taking care of Underdawg. Someone had written (in an uninspired Calibri font):

Vote Cheer for Gardner Hall President

With a picture of Harold front and center.

Election time.

Being a freshman, I had no experience with the process. But from what I'd gathered from 1980's movies and the stories Justin told, elections ran for a couple weeks, during which the candidates made campaign promises that centered around beer, gave speeches about more beer and made boastful, bold claims about how much beer they were capable of drinking.

All pretty harmless stuff—except Harold Cheer's poster didn't have the word "beer" anywhere on it. The words that did litter the page included "Others," "Restrictions" and "Separation."

I couldn't believe it. The kid was running on a platform that Others should be segregated into their own dormitory.

Oh, hell no! I thought as I ripped down one of the posters. *I'm not going to let some little shit with a chip on his shoulder undo the good of this university.* McGill was one of the very few places that welcomed Others, and this shithead was trying to undo it.

No, no, no! I stomped up and down the stairwell, my rage bursting forth in flames like Dante's eighth circle of Hell.

I started ripping down Harold's posters. *This place is a sanctuary. A safe haven. Not some pathetic platform for bigots and racists.*

Once I had removed all the posters I could see, I began ripping them to shreds as I binned them with unbridled fury.

Sorry—not racists, I thought. *Otherists! And the worst thing, the absolute crime of it all, is just because Harold Cheer—stupid name, by the way—is human, he somehow thinks he's entitled to spew this crap.*

Of course, my little rant/tantrum had been out loud. And not just spoken out loud, but—as was my habit when I was truly angry—screamed out loud.

That became painfully clear when a roar of cheers and clapping erupted as I trashed the last poster.

I had an audience. Front and center stood Harold Cheer, holding a stack of posters in his hand and giving me a look that could have frozen a roaring fire pit.

↔

"You can't do that," Harold said in a surprisingly calm tone, given what I had done to his posters.

"Do what?"

"Rip down my posters."

"You call those posters? More like a modern form of Judeo-Bolshevism, only aimed at Others this time," I said. Scanning the crowd, I saw that my little 1935 Nazi propaganda reference flew over most of their heads. I guessed you had to have been in pre-World War II Germany to appreciate the magnitude of my insult. I was there, and my insult was a doozy ... I promise.

"Anti-Other propaganda," I added, and several heads nodded in understanding.

"First of all," Harold said, still cool and in control, "it is not propaganda. It is a proposal. More than a proposal, it is an invitation for debate, discussion and deliberation. Secondly—"

"I hate people who alliterate in speech. So smug, slimy and sad." I hissed every "s."

"Secondly," he said, ignoring my insult, "you must acknowledge that Other culture often clashes with ours. Take your changeling roommate—always prancing around naked, stapling AstroTurf to the walls ... and not to mention those baby rats she bottle-fed."

"You know about that?" I asked. The rest of the stuff was undeniable. Deirdre had many fine qualities, but being discreet wasn't one of

27

them. That said, I thought we'd gotten away with the whole rat pups debacle.

Harold nodded. "That, and much more. But it's not just her. There's Sal in McConnell Hall and his apu ways, or Kaito and his massive ... ahem ... you know."

"Balls," I offered. Kaito was a tanuki from pre-Buddhist tradition. At one point, he and his fellow tanuki were the lord judges of the divine. In other words, if you had a problem, you went to a tanuki to preside over the case. They were so well-respected that their ruling was final. Tanuki looked like raccoons, with one vital exception: they had testicles the size of a MINI Cooper.

I guess you have to have big balls when passing laws that affect the universe.

Of course, that was a long time ago, and Kaito was now just a rodent with unseemly boy bits studying human law.

"Yes ... 'balls,' as you so crudely put it. Why should we suffer the sight of them just because—"

"He was born that way. I don't know, Harold, I suffer the sight of you and the poor skin condition your bad genes gave you."

It was a low blow, and probably not helping my case—but hey, I was angry. Besides, when a kid with bright, almost bug-like eyes cried out, "Hear, hear," I felt somehow vindicated.

Harold touched the fresh, volcanic zit on his chin before shaking his head. "Whatever. You can insult me as much as you like, but it doesn't change the fact that I'm allowed to run for Gardner Hall's president on any platform I choose. You owe me posters."

I pulled out my purse and slammed twenty bucks into his hand. "And it doesn't change the fact that I can run against you on a platform of inclusivity and hope." At this, the crowd erupted in cheers, clapping and hoots.

When the cheering died down, Harold gave me a smile as cool as slime on the surface of a swamp and looked at his watch. "You can't. Deadline to put your name in the running expires in ... three, two, one. Time's up." He showed me his watch, which read 10am.

"Actually," a voice called from behind, "she's fine. I put her name in ten minutes ago."

Scanning the crowd to see who was speaking, I spotted Andrew Garner holding up a paper, his black fingernail polish a sharp contrast to the form declaring my candidacy.

I guess I really am running for hall president, I thought with a sigh.

6

WALKING, TALKING AND ROCKING

*H*arold stormed off in a huff. Given the crowd's reaction to my words, I was going to beat him and he knew it. Score one for the good guys. Now I just had to figure out what the president's responsibilities were.

I'd do that later. Now, I needed to get down to the library and research. Andrew walked over to me and handed me a copy of the application. "Here," he said, "you should probably have this."

"Ahh, thanks," I said. "That was quick thinking on your part."

"Yeah well, I had no idea you were going to get into it with him when I put in your application. I went over to admin and submitted it after I saw you ripping down the posters. Figured if you're that pissed, I could convince you to run for sure."

"How so?"

"No one gets angry like you did and doesn't want to put people in their place. I'm the same way. I see a smug look on someone's face and all I want to do is take 'em down, if you know what I mean."

I did, not that I said anything. I just nodded.

"So us being kindred spirits and all, I thought I'd put your name in."

"Good foresight."

"Hmph. It's what I do," he said while flicking back his blond hair.

He was all right; I had no idea why Cassy would give him such a cold shoulder. "So," he said after a long pause, "you'll need a campaign manager."

"And let me guess … you know just the right long-haired, black-nail-polish-wearing guy for the job."

"At your service," he said with a surprisingly crisp and proper salute.

↔

Faster than you could say "Underdawg" three times, the crowd dispersed with a few students giving me a thumbs-up and a couple even going so far as to shake my hand.

If I were a normal human girl, determined to make the grade and get that fantastic job after graduation, I'd consider this move a check in the *plus* column. But the truth was, I had plenty of money, a castle just outside Inverness, Scotland, and enough antiques I could sell off in a pinch to any museum in the world.

In other words, I had every reason to coast, and being hall president during the day and vigilante by night was just the kind of overachieving people like me avoided.

Still, someone needed to put Cheer in his place. And given the platform he planned to run on, I wanted to be the person to do it. I guess my desire not to overachieve was being overrun by my need to do what I believed to be right.

Yay me. It was going to be an exhausting year—a fact I lamented as I made my way down the hill. I had wanted to think things through, figure out what my ever-growing list of priorities was, but Andrew insisted on walking to campus with me.

In his words, we needed to hash out the campaign strategy.

"I think the strategy is to simply crush our opponents beneath our ever-righteous boot," I said.

Either Andrew didn't get my joke or wasn't in the mood, because he just shook his head. "Righteousness doesn't poll well. We need a more tactful strategy. What are our assets?" He leered at me, examining me from ankle to forehead. I'd think he was perving on me, except I was wearing waterproof clothing. You can't be sexy in waterproof clothing—that has been scientifically proven.

"OK," he finally settled, "you are cooler, better looking and more charismatic than he is …"

"A jaundiced mule is cooler, better looking and more charismatic than Cheer. Your point?"

"My point is that—"

"Look Andrew, I'm sure I'll just get up in front of the crowd, yell some sensible stuff that isn't filled with Other-hating rhetoric and win the day." My mind went back to the crowd and how supportive they'd been of everything I'd said. If that crowd was any indication of the electoral process, I would be a shoo-in.

Andrew stopped walking, and I had taken about three steps before I realized he was no longer in stride with me. I turned to see the blond, six-foot-three boy looking down at me with utter confusion painted across his face. "You don't get it," he finally said, not so much as a judgement, but as if stating a fact.

"Get what?"

"You think the handful of students cheering you on represents everyone on campus, don't you?"

"Well?"

"Gardner Hall is an anomaly. The other halls—Molson, McConnell, Douglas, Solin, RVC—they're not Gardner."

"And what makes Gardner so special?"

"First of all, it's the only hall with a 30% ratio of Others in residence. The other halls have 10% at best."

"Which means …"

"Which means Gardner is more used to Others than the rest of the halls. Which means that just because Gardner will vote for Other rights, doesn't mean the other halls will. I mean, it was only a few months ago that Dr. Dewey was killed—"

"By a human."

He lifted a curious eyebrow. "We don't know who killed Dr. Dewey. The killer was never caught. And let's not forget what happened just two days after he died—the flying jinn and that crazy woman who tried to sacrifice McGill's student body to the gods."

I was being so stupid I could have punched myself in the nose. Dr. Dewey was an old librarian (and the first friend I made on campus) who had been ritually murdered by a human who thought the gods left because humans had abandoned their old, bloody, human-sacrificing ways.

And, as if murdering Dr. Dewey wasn't enough, she had planned to sacrifice dozens (if not hundreds) of students at the beginning-of-the-year party because she thought she could call the gods back.

With a lot of help, I had managed to stop her before she could hurt anyone else ... but only a handful of us knew who she was and what she'd been up to. The majority of students knew nothing about what had really happened.

I had stopped her while wearing my father's cherub mask. Outside of my friends, no one knew I had a hand in the whole thing. And here I was spouting off that a "human" had killed the librarian, like I knew something he didn't.

For someone who wants to live an anonymous life, I shouldn't like the attention.

"OK," I finally said, "but that's my point: no one knows who killed the librarian. But the crazy woman at the party—she was human. I just figured that she was also the one who killed the librarian."

"Most of us would agree, but that's all speculation. You can't win a presidency based off speculation."

Now it was my turn to lift a confused eyebrow. "I don't know about that—have you been following the U.S. elections?"

He lifted up defensive palms. "OK, you're right. But let me put it this way: you *shouldn't* win an election using speculation. That's not how the world should work." He slammed an angry fist into his left palm.

"Whoa, easy there boy," I said.

"Sorry, I just get so angry." He shuddered like he was trying to shake off the anger. "I'm better now, but my point still stands. Harold—"

"Cheer-*less*."

"Sure, fair enough. Harold Cheer-*less* has supporters. Lots of them. They might not be that vocal—after all, you're kind of an asshole if you say Other-hating stuff out loud—but that doesn't change the fact that most people are assholes and when it comes to a secret ballot, they'll vote along their asshole lines."

He was right: anonymity is the coward's shield. People say and do what they want when they know they won't have to face consequences. Just think mob mentality, closeted racists and internet trolls.

Others had only come onto the scene during the last four years, and humans were still getting used to the idea that their neighbors were a dust of pixies or an angry of dwarves, with all their strange ways. (If you don't believe me, just try negotiating with a dwarf—it is literally a staring contest.)

But the asshole pendulum swung both ways, and some people—pressured by friends or family to be wary of Others—might say one thing but vote another.

That, too, happens.

As it stood, I wasn't completely convinced that Andrew was right. Yes, many were scared, but McGill was the first—and still one of the only—places that accepted Other students. And according to university stats, human enrollment had never been higher.

Still, Andrew has a point. This election should not be won by assuming the best in the people. We should be more purposeful, clear in our messaging and uncompromising in our ideals, I thought.

From the "Yes!" that Andrew gave me, I guessed I thought that out loud. "A bit weird being referred to in the third person when I'm standing right here, but I totally agree."

"Fine," I said, resuming my trek down the hill and toward campus, "what are the next steps?"

"We settle on our platform."

"Isn't that obvious?" I said. "Other rights—as in equal rights."

"Fair enough. I'll work on the phrasing. How about, 'Others shouldn't have *other* rights'? Or, 'Other but equal'?" Andrew churned through a dozen or so slogans as we turned down University Street and passed through the main gate onto campus. We had just gotten to the outskirts of the quad, an open-air area of the lower campus surrounded by two libraries, the Arts building and the Faculty of Engineering.

It was also the place most students gathered to hang out between classes.

"OK," I said, seeing the Other Studies Library across the quad. I wanted to end this conversation so I could work on my other extracurricular activities. "We'll figure out the slogan later. Once that's done, we'll—"

"Print posters, canvas and give speeches. Lots of handshaking and baby kiss—"

"Be wary," a voice said from behind us.

I turned to see Cassy walking up to us. She was walking right toward me. "Be wary," she repeated. "He will—"

But before she could finish, something exploded right in the center of the quad.

7

JUSTICE LEAGUE VS. THE LEAGUE OF DOOM VS. ONE GIRL IN SNOW PANTS

*W*e all want to be superheroes. We might not admit it to anyone, but when we're alone, we all dream of having superpowers and fighting the good fight. Maybe we wouldn't have the grand adventures of Spiderman or make the noir sacrifices of Batman, but super strength, flying, invisibility, the Force ... they're all powers most of us would never turn down.

Until you see them in full effect.

And that's something I have personal experience with: super strength, speed, healing ... all part of the gift basket called vampire-hood. You very quickly (as in almost instantly) stop worrying about the consequences of your actions because, well, there aren't many. After all, who's going to pick a fight with a vamp?

Superpowers also mean you have the souped-up ability to do harm without many of the consequences that go along with having so much power. After all, if you could lift a truck and throw it at someone without fear of being hurt or any reprisal, why not?

Two words: collateral damage.

A girl dressed up like Jessica Jones was standing next to *The Three Bares* statue, screaming at some kid in an orange jumpsuit. He glowed gold as he hovered in the air, and he wore a black belt, a monkey's tail and the Daoist symbol for "turtle" on his left breast.

"Goku?" Andrew said with absent-minded awe.

"Of course," I said, slapping my forehead. "From *Dragon Ball Z.*"

That was all I managed to get out before Jessica Jones picked up some poor workman's maintenance truck—the man paused in his lawn mowing to watch—and threw it at Goku.

Comet Boy slapped the flying truck with the back of his hand and sent it hurtling right at us.

I tackled Cassy and Andrew, narrowly pushing them out of the way. The three of us tumbled into the snowbank, the truck only just missing us as it crashed on the ground and skidded by.

"Phew," I said.

"Oh. My. God," Andrew huffed out, then looked at me. "Thank you, thank you, thank you!"

Cassy, on the other hand, was less than grateful. "You shouldn't have," she muttered, and looking into her ocean blue and gray eyes, I saw she meant it.

Shouldn't have what? Risked my life to save them? Or saved them at all? I wasn't sure what she meant, but I didn't have time to think about that now.

"The engineering building. You guys run in there—now!"

"What about you?" Andrew asked.

Looking at the Jessica Jones look-alike across the field, I shrugged and said, "I gotta go see about a girl."

↔

I waited to make sure that Cassy and Andrew were safely inside before standing up, dusting off the snow on my oh-so-well-fitted outfit and casually making my way toward the quad and the two battling superheroes.

They were staring at each other, Comet Boy hovering like a golden ornament on a Christmas tree. Up close, I saw the girl was wearing black jeans, a black scarf and a black jacket. At this distance, she was less Jessica Jones and more super-strong goth girl (not that there was much of a distinction).

She pointed at the hovering kid. "I'm sick of you following me."

"And I'm sick of you walking away every time we have a fight."

Seriously, I thought, *a lovers' quarrel?*

"Excuse me," she said, "but this is none of your business."

Thinking out loud—again!

"Look," I said, my hands out in a *I mean you no harm* kind of way. I looked around and saw that most people had ducked for cover. A lot of faces were looking at us from windows or behind trees, but there was no one out in the open. As for the groundskeeper, he had run away the second his truck went flying. "Your fight is none of my business, but the truck you tossed up in the air nearly splattered me and two of my friends across the pavement. That kind of is my business."

"She's always throwing shit when she's angry," Comet Boy said.

"Then don't make her angry," I said, looking up at him.

"Thank you!" she cried out.

"And you—don't throw trucks. And what's more—" I started, but a guy wearing what looked like a rhino costume bulldozed over the girl.

"Never fear," Rhino Boy said, "I will take down this campus terror!"

"Hey, that's my girlfriend!" Comet Boy said, immediately diving into Rhino Boy, hitting him so hard that a boy-sized crater was all that remained.

Comet Boy was worse for wear. Apparently, glowing or not, diving into asphalt hurt.

And just when I thought the worst was over, Comet Boy got to his feet, staggering in disorientation, and all kinds of hell erupted.

Well, not hell exactly ... more like all kinds of superpowers collided.

8

SUPERHEROES NEVER THINK ABOUT REPAIR COSTS

Sometimes I wish I had a propensity for exaggeration. Hyperbole, tall tales, a based-on-a-true-story way about me. But I don't, and I guess that's what makes my stories so unbelievable. I tell them as I see them.

And what I saw was at least twenty-one kids with superpowers duking it out.

There was a wide range of superpowers, most inspired by the mad rush of superhero movies we've had over the last few years. Guys with hammers, girls with swords. They were mostly fighting as individuals, but a few of them had teamed up like some sort of weird Justice (or anti-justice) League.

Three girls with impossibly huge eyes flew around in unison (I'm guessing *Powerpuff Girls* fans) as they attacked a kid with blond bangs riding a green and orange tiger.

There was even a scrawny kid with no clothes on except tight purple, ripped jeans. He was green and screaming, "Chad smash!" It was almost comical to see him prancing around—until, that was, he grabbed a lamp post, ripped it out of the ground and used it as a fly swatter to take down the three *Powerpuff*-esque girls.

It was chaos. They were fighting each other like creatures possessed. Frequently one of them would say something like, "Don't hurt my school!" while throwing a piece of said school at another super-powered student.

And what became quickly apparent was that they were defending McGill's campus *with* McGill's campus, and none of them seemed to understand that all the damage would cease as soon as they did.

And the worst part: if they didn't stop soon, there wouldn't be any campus left to defend.

So how do you stop a league of superheroes hell-bent on fighting each other to defend their school?

Give them a common enemy.

↔

I ducked into the arts building and found the closest bathroom to change in (I would've looked for a phone booth, but in this day and age, those weren't really available).

Before going in, I made sure no one saw me. That was an easy feat, given what was going on outside. A part of me wanted to thank them for the distraction, but the more sensible part of me chimed in that I wouldn't need a distraction in the first place if it wasn't for them.

Pulling out my cherub's mask from my bag, I put it on as I took off my winter coat and snow pants. It was going to be cold, but given how much running I was planning on doing, I suspected I'd be glad for the lack of clothing.

Once that was done, I hid my stuff as best as I could. The bathroom was an old building, so there weren't many options besides an old cubby-hole designed to hide pipes and whatnot, which was where I put my stuff. I'd have to get back to it before any maintenance staff needed to get in, but at least it was out of sight for regular peeps who needed the loo.

Once that was done, it was time to do a little bit of destruction myself.

↔

Leaving from a side entrance, I made my way over to the groundskeeper's truck and found exactly what I was looking for: a tile spade. With that in hand, I went to locate a crater with just the right kind of piping for a delicate operation like this one.

Montreal gets as much snow as Siberia, and because the city is guaranteed to get freezing weather conditions, all the piping is beneath the frost line—about six feet under. So to get to any of it, I'd need a hole roughly that deep. Luckily for me, the fight had provided me with plenty of holes to choose from.

Right in the center of the quad were crossroads, and all the fighting had busted up the meeting point of those roads. Several pipes had been unearthed—which was exactly what I was looking for. Dodging Rhino Boy and another kid who I was pretty sure was doing his own take on *Afro Samurai*, I dived into the pit. Tapping the tile spade against the ceramic and metal pipes, I listened for a muted thud. When I found it, I drove the narrow end of the shovel hard into the pipe.

I didn't have super strength, so I had to hit it hard a couple times until I got the desired result … a geyser of warm water that shot up into the sky. The heat hit the cool Montreal air with a whoosh, creating a volcano of water and steam.

It looked much worse than it was, which was exactly what I was going for.

Twenty-one superheroes stopped fighting and looked at me. We stood in a peaceful stance (well, peaceful if you ignored the rush of water and steam) for about three seconds before Comet Boy pointed at me and yelled, "Get her!"

. . .

... End of Part 1

PART II
INTERMISSION

Everyone dreams of glory: belting out that perfect ballad, scoring the winning goal, money and splendor, fame and heroism. It's human nature to covet grandeur in the safe and private confines of our mind.

And when the mood of fantasy and fancy takes us, we also dream of powers beyond the capacity of a normal human. For who among us has not dreamt of flying, super strength, or perhaps the martial prowess of ninja, samurai, spies, or all three?

In other words, we all dream of being spectacular, powerful ... super.

We dream of the high adventure allowed by unearned powers suddenly and inexplicably granted. That is the stuff of many a harmless daydream. Dreams of being the superhero of our own story, the vigilante who saves the day, the white knight who wins the hand of the prince or princess.

These dreams are private, rarely shared, but they are there and serve as one of many threads that bind us together and define us as human.

We all dream of being superheroes, and Mary Carnahan, Russell Brandford and Ellen Scovil are no exception.

Mary wants to be a reporter, and after watching the Netflix series *Jessica Jones*, thinks to herself, "How cool would it be to be just like that badass detective?"

She looks over at her boyfriend, Dustin Riley, who is watching *Dragon Ball Z* for the umpteenth time on his laptop and she so desperately wants to *kamehameha* the laptop out the window.

Russell is reading up on grimoires and spells and all kinds of ancient magic. He loves the stuff, and wants to ask the południca who runs the 24 hour depanneur on Pine Street if she knows any magic herself.

Ellen is alone her room, trying to work up the courage to tell the boys next door to shut their damn stereo off. But she can't muster the bravery and, putting on the noise-cancelling earphones her mom bought her, surfs YouTube. A *ThunderCats* video appears in her feed. Clicking on it, she giggles to herself. "I remember this cartoon. What was the name of the female lead? Oh yeah—Cheetara. She was badass. She wouldn't have any trouble telling those boys to shut up."

And so, they—and many others—dream. Superheroes and superpowers. Unearned abilities. High adventure. Something, anything to free them from the day-to-day.

But alas, superheroes don't exist, and superpowers are something only Others have—and those powers come at a high cost.

So Mary, Russell and Ellen go to sleep expecting to wake up the next morning exactly as they have always been: normal kids, sans superpowers.

That was the night before. The next morning brings with it something very different, for before any of them can step out of bed, they all realize that they are no longer normal.

Not anymore.

Flexing muscles she didn't know she had, Ellen growls like a cheetah ...

Mary jumps out of bed and cracks her concrete ceiling ...

And as for Russell ... Russell can control time itself.

Who said dreams can't come true?

9

RUN, LOLA ... AHH, I MEAN ... RUN, KAT, RUN

*E*ver been rushed by a bunch (power?) of superheroes? I have, and this was after I had to overcome my belief that super-heroes weren't real. The twenty-plus superheroes all charged me, temporarily forgetting that only moments ago, they were at each other's throats.

Luckily, I had anticipated this. I rolled out of the way and made my way off campus and toward the city of Montreal.

It was nearly impossible to outrun people with super strength and speed—that was, when they knew their limitations. But I could tell from the uncoordinated way they battled each other and their haphazard attempts to hurt one another that these guys were new to the whole superpowers thing.

I remembered being a newly made vampire. Simple tasks like holding a glass or lifting a bag were troublesome, and usually resulted in the glass shattering or the bag flying into the air.

So when the heroes charged at me, I tumbled away at the last second, causing them to shoot past me and crash into whatever happened to be in front of them. I ran toward stones, blocks, walls and heavy oak trees, some of which vaporized in my wake.

I could practically smell the ozone.

45

And the slower heroes who shot energy balls or threw stuff at me would always miss. They often hit the others, which ultimately helped me escape.

All of that is what brought me, still alive, to the James McGill statue about a hundred feet from the exit. But the statue wasn't very big and, small as I was, didn't offer much cover. I needed a miracle to escape and, well, miracles were in short supply these days.

But not friggin' gorgeous girls with silver hair and eyes that could melt you in place. Just as three of the superheroes were lining up their energy balls and flying hammers and whatever the hell else superheroes shoot innocent vigilantes with, Cassy jumped between James McGill and me—and the superheroes—with her arms spread like a human shield or something.

The three superheroes stopped at once, just staring down at her as she glared at them defiantly. "This isn't how this works," she growled. "Superheroes protect each other—not chase after girls like greyhounds after a rabbit."

I stirred from behind the statue and the three superheroes' eyes darted toward me. Cassy, still in her protective stance, looked over her shoulder at me and yelled, "RUN!"

↔

She didn't need to tell me twice. I ran out of McGill's main gate and down two blocks to a shopping mall called the Eaton Center. It was my best bet for losing them. Taking only a second to look back, I realized I'd only managed to make it this far without being splattered because Cassy was doing her best to block their path. Superheroes or not, they didn't want to hurt Cassy.

Most of them ran around her, a few stopped to talk—possibly flirt with her—but whatever their response to Cassy's human shield*ieness*, she had bought me enough time to make it this far.

Still, there were a bunch of them after me as I ducked into the Eaton Center.

↔

Another cool feature of Montreal is what you can't see from the street. Because it's so cold for so much of the year, you can get from one end of the city to the other completely underground. I'm not talking subways, although those exist. I'm talking basement levels to the businesses and shopping centers that have underground exits and entrances into each other.

I made my way to the Eaton's Center basement. I had somehow managed to lose most of the twenty-one. Only three seemed to be hot on my scent—a young lady who looked a lot like Cheetara from *Thun-derCats* and two guys wearing identical red spandex, each with a lightning bolt on his chest.

The two red spandex guys were so unsure of their footing that they slipped and slid on the shopping center's polished floors. Still, they were so fast that every time I tripped them up, they found their footing and were on me in a flash.

I needed to change tactics, but first I had to get those three off my tail. First, a distraction.

Up in the men's section, I grabbed several leather belts, and as I ran, laced two of them together until they formed a chain. Then, using an old trick I learned from a rancher in Montana, I snared the two boys together, temporarily hobbling them.

Cheetah Girl—who was still entering the shop—jumped at me, just as I knew she would. I tumbled backward into a clothing rack and wrapped the third belt around her neck and the base of the rack.

The snares wouldn't last for long. Nearby, the two boys were already breaking free (and probably would have already if they weren't fumbling with their own supersonic fingers). I had bought myself a few seconds to lay the next trap.

Running into the perfume department, I grabbed every bottle I could find and smashed them on the ground. Chanel, Obsession for men and women, Bright Crystal Absolu, Victoria's Secret Bombshell, Lancôme Trésor Midnight Rose and Dior Poison Girl. They all permeated the air, thus throwing Cheetah Lady off my scent.

The two girls at the counter ran out as soon as they saw a weirdo in a kilt and cherub mask. And when the two mall security guards ran in a few seconds later, I only needed to show them my dirk and they turned on their heels and ran out.

That done, I moved a massive poster of Charlize Theron looking all sultry and seductive as she advertised J'Adore by Dior so I could hide while still having a good view of the room. I waited for the two super-fast kids to make their way into the perfume department.

Ever see that scene in *Jurassic Park* when the Tyrannosaurus rex's approach is announced by the ripples in a glass of water? Well, the two super-fast kids weren't prehistoric dinosaurs with massive heads and teeny tiny arms, but their arrival was announced nonetheless.

Not in water, but in the pool of perfume I had created. It started with tiny little ripples, but because the guys were lightweight and so incredibly fast, their vibrations shocked the ground so that the tiny ripples turned into little droplets that jumped out of the pool. The closer they got, the more the puddle of perfume looked like a thousand ball bearings dancing on a canvas of linoleum.

As soon as I was certain the two of them were close, I came out from around Charlize Theron. "Yoohoo! Looking for me?"

The two of them *flashed* over to me. I needed to time this perfectly if I was going to get away, so before the word "me" left my lips, I leapt onto the counters and up, grabbing one of the sprinklers jutting from the ceiling.

My timing was perfect. My plan, not so much.

The two boys crashed into Charlize Theron, knocking the poor woman over, and before they realized what was going on, they slid helplessly on the perfume pool and into the very real and solid concrete pillar behind the poster. The two kids knocked themselves out just as I had anticipated.

What I hadn't counted on was them being so fast that the friction from their steps would ignite the perfume. The floor went up in flames, causing the sprinkler I was holding to erupt in water.

And for the second time that day, I was wet and cold.

10
STILL UNDERGROUND, STILL SCREWED

I needed to find a way to change—and if not change, then at the very least ditch my cherub mask away from the prying eyes of security cameras. I had to find a place to hide, and I thought I knew just the place.

Heading through the Eaton Center, I found the underground passage that led under McGill Street and into the Cineplex Odeon complex. There was an Indigo bookstore next to the cinema, and I figured I could probably steal a tote bag to hide my mask, and then use some of the back *Staff Only* passageways to break into the cinema. I could duck into a movie and wait for all of this to cool off, walk out with my mask hidden and make my way back to campus (before I froze my butt off) to get my coat and snow pants.

I figured I didn't have to worry about police. After all, they had a bunch of superheroes to worry about before they'd chase after some girl that scared off a couple counter attendants and mall security by waving a knife.

Then again, maybe they would come after me, thinking I was a superhero myself. I could be pretty menacing, after all. Either way, I had two choices: go back and hope that Cheetah Girl was still running around blind (well, nose-blind, at least) and that the two fast kids were still unconscious, or go forward. I wasn't about to risk dealing with them again, so this was my only option.

Not the best plan, but I didn't have any money or a phone, so it was probably the only option I had. That, or send telepathic signals to Egya or Deirdre to come pick me up. But since my human brain could no longer do that, I was fresh out of options.

Getting into the store was easy enough, as was stealing the bag. And as for the *Staff Only* passageways, humans should really start tightening their security. It was amazing the kind of access you had when you weren't worrying about *No Entry* signs, or whether you were on salary.

I found a back tunnel that led to a room that connected to the fire exit for one of the Odeon Multiplex screens. Sneaking in, I found myself watching some Hollywood special effects monstrosity. And since it was the smack dab middle of the afternoon, there was hardly anyone there. Just a few kids who, judging by how zealously they ate their popcorn, were probably stoned.

Phew, I thought as I plopped myself in a seat in the front row. *I made it.*

Not bad for a human girl. Hell, not bad for a vampire. Not bad at all. Took on the Justice League and League of Doom at the same time … and I lived to fight another day. Not bad at all.

Ahh, hubris, thy ways are cruel. Just before I could remove my mask and settle into my seat to get lost in whatever movie was playing, I heard a *swoosh*, followed by what can only be described as extremely sticky Silly Putty latching onto my bag and pulling it straight up.

↔

I looked up and saw a guy hanging upside down from the ceiling. He was pulling up my stolen tote bag using string attached to his wrist. When he saw nothing in the tote, he let it drop.

"Let me guess. Spider—"

"Guy. Spider Guy—that's me," he said.

What is it with these guys personalizing their superhero identities? I thought ... sadly out loud.

Spider Guy, who wore a red bandana over his head and a second one over his face, narrowed his eyes as if he didn't understand the question. Then he shrugged. "Copyright issues? Or maybe I've just gotta be me." He pointed a finger at me and I expected more sticky silly string to shoot out, but instead he just waggled it. "Say, you're the girl from the party."

"What party?" I asked, moving my hand down to my dirk.

"The one where that psycho tried to sacrifice a bunch of us. As in, ritually. You saved us."

I nodded, which isn't the easiest thing to do when you're looking straight up.

"I always wondered about you. You kind of just disappeared after that. I mean, there were rumors of sightings, but nothing concrete. Still, you saved us. You're a hero." He was fumbling for something at his waist. "I thought you were on our side, but now I'm not so sure. After all, if you really are a hero, why did you do what you did?"

"What's that?" I asked.

"Damage the campus," he said. He lifted what he had been reaching for and put it to his mouth. When it produced an audible click, I realized it was a walkie-talkie. "I got her. She's in screen 3."

Oh, crap! He was calling in reinforcements.

↔

"Can't we just call it even?" I said. "I saved you, remember? What's a little damage given all that?"

Spider Guy didn't respond, the walkie-talkie still in his hand.

"Come on," I cried out. "We don't have to do this. Like you said, I'm on your side."

Nothing.

"At least answer me. You owe me that much."

Still nothing.

I looked toward the upper rows where the stoned kids were sitting. Either they hadn't noticed our little chat, hadn't cared, or thought it was part of the show. Whatever it was, they didn't react. As in not at all, and it was then that I understood what was going on. The stoned kids weren't just not reacting—their hands were frozen mid-popcorn grab.

And as for Spider Guy, he wasn't answering me because he *couldn't*. He was frozen, which meant one of two things: either something had paralyzed him and the stoner kids ... or time was frozen.

I'd never seen this kind of magic before, but I'd heard of it. It was referred to as the Hunter's Mark, a spell so powerful that legend speaks of only the Earl King (master hunter and all around bad, bad dude!) having the power to use it.

According to legend, the Hunter's Mark was deployed to create the perfect hunting conditions. The Earl King would stop time for everyone save himself and his prey. Then the true hunt would begin between just the two of them.

There was more to the legend, but I didn't have time to try and recall it all now. Now, I needed to run.

Except in my confusion and desire to barter with Spider Guy, I had wasted too much time. (Look at me, *wasting too much time* with time frozen? Oh, the irony. I just hoped I would live long enough to tell someone about it.)

I turned to run out through the exit I had entered by, only to be met by a guy wearing a child's wizardry robe. I mean, the thing was covered in stars, shooting comets and crescent moons.

"You're not the Earl King," I said.

"I am not!" the kid bellowed. "I am the great Grimoire Keeper, and in my possession are ancient tomes that hold the secrets of the universe."

The kid pulled out a large leather book that was almost too cumbersome for him to manage and flipped through the pages. I had just enough time to read the cover: *München Handbuch der Dämonischen Magie* ... also known as the Necromancer's Manual.

Holy guacamole, I thought. *That's no copy. If this kid has the original manual and can use its magic, he could become the most powerful being on this planet.*

"Why, thank you," the kid said as he flipped through the pages.

I knew I should be running, but I couldn't help myself. That manual wasn't just dangerous ... it was like giving the kid access to the nuclear codes and putting an *I dare you* sign over the button.

"Kid, where did you get that?"

Kid Wizard—I couldn't think of what else to call him—smiled. "I've always been into this kind of stuff. You know, myths and magic, and I've always wanted to be a sorcerer, but when the gods left and took their magic with them, I figured that dream was gone. Then poof,"—he smiled, still scanning his pages—"I woke up yesterday morning and this grimoire was on my bedside. And I could read it."

He flipped through four more pages before saying, "Ahh yes, here we go."

He started moving his hands around, chanting in Latin mixed with Draugr and Gnomish ...

"Kid," I said, "you don't want to do that."

Kid Wizard ignored me, his incantation growing louder before he threw an open palm in my direction and screamed, *"Fuego!"*

Nothing happened.

He looked at me, puzzled. "Hold on, I should have shot a fireball at you."

"I know, kid," I said taking three steps forward. "You should have, but the thing about the Hunter's Mark is, it was about leveling the battleground between the Earl King and the thing—or person—he was hunting. That means no other hunters, no hounds to help him and *no magic.*"

I pulled back my fist and punched Kid Wizard square in the nose. He fell like a poorly stacked *Jenga* tower. Grabbing the grimoire and throwing it in my tote bag, I ran for the exit.

"Hold on!" Spider Guy cried out as the stoner kids started laughing.

Evidently if you break a wizard's nose, you break their spell, too.

11

SUPERHEROES TO MY LEFT, SUPERHEROES TO MY RIGHT

*R*unning back down the maintenance hallway, I tried to formulate a plan. They'd be on me in a few seconds and I honestly had no idea what I could do. What's more, I didn't know what they'd do to me when they caught me. Beat me up? Take me to the authorities? Kill me?

When I spoke to them they seemed pretty rational, but that kid wizard literally tried to throw a fireball at me. Either he didn't know how deadly such magic was or didn't care. Or maybe he just wanted to throw a fireball and see what it did.

Whatever his thoughts on the matter, he could have killed me. There was something strange going on, too: they were too rational to be homicidal when they spoke, and too homicidal to be rational when they acted.

I ran to the end of the hall and had almost gotten to the exit when I felt something strike my ankle and pull at me. I was yanked back to the middle of the hall, where Spider Guy and three other heroes jumped over me to block the exit to my right. I considered running to my left and back to the cinema when four more superheroes poured out of the doorway.

"Ahh guys, are you sure you want to do this?"

Several of them shrugged before charging me. I didn't have time to think, so I just reacted by pulling out my dirk. I was ready to fight for keeps this time.

I was just about to stick the pointy end of my blade into Spider Guy's throat when a large, heavy blanket was thrown over me.

A guy dressed in all black was under there with me. Well, more like on top of me. I could feel the kicks and punches of the super-heroes wailing on the blanket before the boy on top of me said, "Hold onto me."

"Wha—?" I started, but before I could say or do anything, he grabbed me with his right arm and held me to one side. Throwing his left arm up and away from us, I felt a wave of energy burst out of him in all directions.

The heavy blanket tore into a million little fragments as the wall in front of and behind us crumbled, holes bursting open to expose the wiring and piping behind them.

And as for the superheroes to our right and left, they went flying in both directions down the hall.

"Phew," the boy said, "I wasn't sure that would work."

I got a look at the guy for the first time and my jaw nearly crashed down to my Dubarry Galway knee-high boots. "Justin," I finally managed.

"In the flesh," my boyfriend said with a not entirely ungraceful curtsy.

↔

"Kinetic blast?"

"Just like Black Panther," he said.

"No," I said, shaking my head, "just like what we were discussing last night. Your superhero powers, the ones you said you wanted—they've manifested themselves."

Justin nodded.

"And you're not worried that you suddenly have powers when just yesterday you didn't?"

He shook his head. "No, not really."

"And you don't find that odd?"

He shrugged. And that reaction was enough for me to know something was truly off. Justin was many things—calm, collected, the ideal guy to have around in a fire—but never unquestioning. No, that wasn't him.

I didn't have time to consider any of that, though. We had to get away. Looking up and down the hall, I saw that not everyone had been knocked out. Some of them were coming around. "Justin, did the other power you wanted also manifest?"

"Oh yeah," he said, grabbing my hand, "it did in all kinds of ways."

↔

He grabbed my hand and in an instant, we were both invisible. It's an odd sensation, not being able to see yourself. It made me realize how much we take our bodies for granted.

At any given moment, our peripheral vision clocks our hands or arms, sometimes even our feet. We *see* our eyelids with every blink, we get a sense of where our limbs go when we move about. We even see our own noses, although most of us have tuned that jutting piece of flesh completely out.

But when you're invisible, all that goes away. No arms or legs or fingers or anything else waving about.

No eyelids to block our vision, if only for a fraction of a second. And no nose to get our bearings with.

Walking would be a challenge, so Justin and I, hand in hand, took it real slow as we made our way past the knocked-over heroes. As we closed in on three of them, I realized I recognized Spider Guy after all. He was the kid who had yelled "Hear, hear" when I was chewing out Harold Cheer.

What the hell was going on?

But that wasn't the only thing that was interesting. Looking over the three fallen heroes, I saw that none of them had aged. Not at all, which meant that somehow they were tapping into all this magic and not sacrificing a second of time.

This was impossible. Ever since the gods left, there had been a steep penalty for using magic: time. Every fireball, every moment spent hanging from a ceiling or shooting out webbing from your wrists—all of it cost time. And not just a bit of it. Lots.

They all should have aged, but Spider Guy was as youthful as he had been this morning, before he went on his magical rampage.

It just didn't make any sense.

We stepped over them and out the door. Once we were back in the bookstore, we made our way outside and back onto campus.

By the time we got there, the campus had been closed. Given how much snow we'd had over the last couple weeks, you'd think we were having a snow day instead of a superhero day (I know, I know, not very funny—but I'm hilarious in Elvish. Really, I am.)

The police had run yellow tape across the entrance while two guards stood nervously at the threshold. I could see from their eyes that if a superhero showed up, they'd bolt. As we passed by, I heard one of the policemen mutter, "Damn Others."

"Amen," said the other.

Jerks! They had no idea what was going on and they were already blaming Others. I was about to let go of Justin's hand and fly into a rage in front of their ignorant asses. That sure would've scared the bejesus out of them.

But I didn't. As it turns out, three hundred years of life gives you a lot of opportunities to practice keeping your cool. Sometimes I even succeeded. Instead of blowing up, I took a deep breath and reminded myself that humans saw magic as something only Others could do. As far as those two cops were concerned, superpowers were akin to magic—hence, Others.

Those cops had been scared. And given their limited knowledge, of course they'd blame Others. Who else was around to point a judging finger at? My only fear now was that the super brats would do something monumentally stupid and Others would get rounded up as a result. Not that I could worry about that now.

Invisible, we passed them and headed to the arts building so I could retrieve my jacket and snow pants.

Justin un-invisiblatized us and as soon as he was in sight, he winked at me. "See, told you I could be useful."

"Stand still," I said, grabbing his head.

Expecting a kiss, he puckered up. But I didn't kiss him. Instead, I carefully examined every millimeter of his face. I looked for signs of crows' feet around his eyes, blotches on his cheeks, skin tags on his neck. Anything that indicated aging.

But like Spider Boy, he was fine. Being a superhero didn't seem to age him one bit.

"You're fine," I said with a bit of disappointment.

"Excuse me?" He narrowed his eyes.

"Sorry. You're fine!" I repeated with more enthusiasm this time. "It's just that you shouldn't be. You should be older. You know, given the whole time-for-magic thing."

"Yeah, sure, but whatever is happening to me … maybe it's an exception to the rule."

I looked up at my perfect, impossibly handsome but very human boyfriend. In my experience, human beings just didn't get how magic works. I sighed. "This isn't a case of A, E, I, O, U and *sometimes* Y. There are rules to magic that can never, ever be broken. That's just the way it works, and it's part of the reason why Others struggle to live in the GoneGod World."

Justin gave me a *go on* gesture.

"Humans grow up learning that there are always exceptions to the rule. In grammar, in spelling, even in mathematics. Of course, they extrapolate that to day-to-day life, too. The rules say the term paper's deadline is Friday, but given the right circumstances, you can get an extension. No one is allowed to cut in line, but if you're disabled or have a young child, then by all means cut to the front. Exceptions.

"But Others have grown up in a world where there are no exceptions. There might be new rules set, like when the gods left and added restrictions to how magic works. But those are new rules, not exceptions. You guys shouldn't be able to do all you did without aging. It simply isn't possible."

"Oh come on," Justin said, and I knew what was coming: *"But magic is in the human world now, so ..."* or *"There are always exceptions, and just because you don't know of any doesn't mean they're not there ..."*

But before Justin could give the typical human objections to the no-exceptions rule of magic, I remembered something from my early days as a vampire.

Or rather, some*one*.

"Justin, can we do that invisibility trick again?" I said. "There's somewhere I'd like to go and its best I'm not seen going there."

12

DAYDREAMS AND FINE ART

*H*idden by Justin's invisibility powers, we made a quick stop at the Other Studies Library so I could gather a couple of supplies I needed to test my theory. That done, we made our way west on Sherbrooke Street, hand in hand.

It was nice. Normally if I wasn't in class or studying, I was vigilante-ing. And when I wasn't doing that, I was usually researching some myth or Other culture or powers to solve some misunderstanding between the once divine creatures and always mundane humans.

I have a lot on my plate and rarely have time for him, I thought. I'm a terrible girlfriend and thank the GoneGods he understands. At least, I think he does. But then again, he's invisible with superpowers, and part of me can't help but think the only reason he has these superpowers is because he wants to spend more time with me.

"For the record," he said, "you're not a terrible girlfriend. You just have weird priorities. And secondly—"

"You heard that?"

"Kat, you think out loud more than you actually speak. I hear a lot."

"Well," I said, feeling my invisible cheeks blush, "you should stop me."

"Why? It's one of your most endearing qualities." I heard his goose-down jacket crinkle as he bent down to kiss me. Given he's six-three and I'm all of five foot nothing, he had a long way to go … which was why he missed my mouth and kissed my ear.

"Yowzer." I stuck a finger in my ear to dry it. "You missed."

"Yeah, ahh, still getting used to where everything is. Being invisible is harder than you'd think."

"Tell me about it," I said, giggling as I held his hand just that little bit tighter. Justin was a good guy. A great guy, and him having powers proved that I wasn't the great gal he deserved.

I wasn't sure how the superhero thing worked, but I was beginning to get an idea. Part of it—the part I was sure of, at least—was desire. Whatever magic was at play here, it fed off certain people's desire to have superpowers. That was the reason why there were only twenty or so superheroes and not hundreds … because these guys were the ones that thought about having powers all the time. Obsessed about it. That's how the magic found them.

And I hated the idea that Justin manifested superpowers just to be with me. The sane, rational part of me knew I shouldn't press this any further, but the insecure, very human part of me needed to ask.

"Justin," I said, trying to soften my tone and be as inviting as I could, "can I ask you a question? About your superpowers? I have a theory as to how this works, and I need to ask you something that might be a wee bit embarrassing. But your answer may clear up a lot about what's going on."

"OK," he said with some trepidation.

"If you don't want to answer me, fine. But if you are going to answer, answer truthfully." I quickly added, "And no matter what you say, no judgment. Promise."

"OK," he repeated. "Shoot." I couldn't see his face, but I knew him well enough to know he was bracing himself for whatever I had in mind.

"Great. Now the truth, OK? How often do you daydream about joining Egya, Deirdre and me on our little missions?"

"Ahh … daydream?"

"Yeah, daydream."

"Well, I think about it a lot."

"No, not *think*. Daydream."

"What's the difference?"

"You can think rationally about something, reason out the pros and cons, but I'm looking for the visualizations. The scenarios that you play out in your mind where you're fighting some Other or perhaps saving me, or—"

"You mean like I did today," he said. "I was pretty rad."

"Rad? That's a throwback."

"Yeah, sorry. I was going through your VHS collection."

I shook my head. He was deflecting—something he did whenever he didn't want to have a certain conversation with me. "Come on Justin," I said. "Focus. How often?"

There was a long pause before he finally said, "Not that much."

"How much?"

There was an audible groan. "I don't know. Every night."

"Every night!" I knew he wanted to join us on our little jaunts, but every night ...

"When?"

"Just before bed."

"You do it every night just before bed."

Another long pause before his voice cracked with, "Yeah. Is that bad?"

"Where?" I asked.

"Usually in the bathroom or while hanging out in your room or mine ..."

"Every night," I repeated.

"Does it help that I'm always thinking of you?"

I nearly pulled my hand away, but remembered that I'd suddenly become visible if I did. Given we were on Sherbrooke in the middle of the day, that was sure to scare the villagers.

We walked on for a bit before he broke the silence. "Is that bad?"

No judgement, I thought (in my head, thankfully). I shook my head before I remembered he couldn't see me. "No. It's just surprising, that's all."

"How so?"

"I didn't think my nighttime extracurricular activities bothered you so much."

"Who said anything about bothering me?" Justin said in a tone that he often used when we were arguing and he'd just realized we were fighting about two different things.

"Clearly it does. If you think about it every night—"

"And sometimes during the day when I'm walking to class. I daydream about joining you guys and fighting the good fight."

We were passing a (visible) couple on the street, and I lowered my voice to a whisper. "This isn't a cartoon. We get hurt. We hurt others, too. And sometimes people die."

Justin started whispering, too. "Yeah, I know. But you're doing it to keep the peace, right? To stop all the tension between Others and humans from bubbling over. I mean, not in the world, but on campus at least."

"That's the goal, but we're really just reacting to shit that happens. Like the ghouls. Deirdre noticed a lot of freshly dug graves on one of her nature walks. We investigated, realized that they were eating the recently dead and we chose to engage them quietly before it escalated to pitchforks and tiki torches."

"So you're doing good."

"Well, in that case Underdawg saved the day. But yes, we're trying."

"So what's so wrong with me wanting to help do good, too? And who knows—if my powers stick around, maybe I can help more often."

We had come to an empty stretch of the sidewalk, and I slowed us a little. "Justin, you know I'm going to do everything I can to get rid of these superheroes. It's no good and will lead to more harm than anything. The way they went after each other—and me—proves that this will only lead to harm."

"I know, but even without superpowers, maybe I could help. I mean, why not?"

I was about to say, "Because you're only human," but held my tongue. That argument wasn't going to get me anywhere. I was only human now, too. But the difference was I had three hundred years of experience as a vampire and hunter. I understood how to react in life and death situations ... but if I was honest with myself (and that was something I was really trying to be these days) it was more than that.

I wasn't afraid to hurt back. It takes a lot of willpower to hurt someone. I mean, really hurt them. And I'm not talking about the I-just-got-punched-and-in-blind-fury-attack-back kind of hurt. I'm talking the premeditated, on purpose, game over, intentional kind of hurt. It's not easy.

It takes practice. Three hundred years of it.

Deirdre was a warrior changeling. She knew all about hurting others.

And as for Egya, he was an ex-were-hyena. I wasn't sure how old he was, but from the way he carried himself, I guessed he was at least a couple hundred years old.

But Justin. He was a normal, nineteen-year-old boy who grew up in a nice neighborhood with loving parents and two dogs. He didn't even like violent video games. He would have no idea how to hurt anyone. He'd only react to being hurt ... and just reacting in a life-and-death fight rarely ended in life.

I couldn't risk him.

Partly because I cared for him.

Mostly because, after centuries of hurting and killing people, I didn't ever want to be responsible for another innocent human being hurt again.

I shook my head and did something I regretted with every newly made human part of me. I lied. "Yeah, maybe you can help. We'll see."

But I wasn't lying to him. I was lying to myself, because part of me wanted him to join us. To be a part of the team, and I thought he just might be able to do it. I knew I was lying to myself, and to him.

I could have backtracked right then and there, but he squeezed my hand as he suppressed what I could assume was a "Yippee." I thought about saying something else to him, tempering his excitement, managing expectations—you know, all the stuff you do when letting someone down easy—but instead I took the coward's way out and said nothing.

Besides, we didn't have time. We had arrived at our destination: the Museum of Fine Arts.

13

THE CURSE OF ART

*A*cross the street from the Museum of Fine Arts is a statue of an angel-like creature with a hole in its chest and several hands piling on top of one another for a face. It's called *The Eye*, though I've never been sure why. The creature doesn't have a single eye anywhere in sight. But eyes notwithstanding, I love this statue. And although I have yet to meet an angel with hands for a face, I believe one must exist.

After all, this GoneGod World is filled with so much diversity and strangeness, how can one not? I have no idea what the artist intended when he designed *The Eye*. All I know is that this marvel of modern art was made before the gods left and the Others came. I like to think that whatever the artist's intention, a part of him saw into the future, saw the coming of the once divine, now mortal creatures, and built this angel to welcome them to our world.

Wishful thinking, I know, but isn't that the point of art? To find meaning and comfort? Or, if not that, a little bit of solace.

So in keeping with a ritual I'd developed whenever I passed by *The Eye*, I touched its toe for good luck before we crossed the street and invisibly walked into the museum.

↔

Inside, we made our way to our destination: the exhibit of Cursed Items. It was an exhibit that simultaneously celebrated the diversity of the GoneGod World while scaring the bejesus out of onlookers.

To sum up the exhibit in a few words would be like trying to describe orange to a blind person, or the sensation of flying to those without wings. Relic after relic sat on display, and although I didn't recognize most of them, I knew enough about the exhibit to know that each relic was a cursed item. And each display was an artistic representation of that curse in play.

A deck of cards that always dealt its owner a losing hand sat on a poker table. A mannequin representing its owner sat head in hands, sobbing.

A hand mill that always spoiled the wheat in it sat in a display of molding bread.

A cup that poisoned anyone who drank from it—no matter how well it was cleaned or what was put in it—sat on a table above several "dead bodies."

And finally, a cupboard with a terrified mannequin trying to run away.

Bingo.

↔

The dybbuk box was one evil artifact. It was the home of an evil spirit that poisoned the box's owners with nightmares and disease. But unlike most cursed items, this thing was doubly cursed. Once for the box's owners, and once for the demon that lived inside.

Invisible, and with Justin's hand in mine, I pulled him close and

69

past the velvet rope that divided onlookers from one of the evilest beings in existence. I swear to the GoneGods, humans do not fear these kinds of things nearly enough.

"Justin," I said, "I need you to put your hand on my shoulder and keep us invisible."

I felt a heavy hand crawl up my arm until it found my shoulder. "Done."

"OK, and I can't emphasize this enough: no matter what happens, don't let go of my shoulder, and don't do or say anything."

"OK."

That was it: OK. *OK?* If he understood where we were and who we were about to wake up, he'd say a lot more than OK. But he didn't know and I wasn't sure how much I should tell him.

Clasping his hand in both of mine, I looked up at where I imagined his face was. "Justin, I cannot emphasize how important it is that you remain quiet. She can't know you're with me."

"OK, Kat. I get it. You don't need to keep repeating yourself. I'm a big boy, and I can keep my mouth shut."

He's right, I thought.

"Thank you," he said.

"No—that was meant to be a private thought. And if you had let me finish, I would have added, 'He's right, but being right doesn't make him safe.' And given who we're about to see—"

"Who?"

"A demon made from nightmares."

"Ha-ha," he chuckled. "That should go on a movie poster or a—"

"No Justin, I'm not kidding, exaggerating or using an expression. This demon is literally made from nightmares. Literally," I repeated, emphasizing each syllable.

There was silence, but from the way his hand moved, I could tell he was trying to see something or—

"Says here the demon is trapped in the box."

—or read something. "Yes, the demon is trapped in the box, but that doesn't make her powerless. In a very real way, she is more powerful in the box than outside it."

"I don't understand."

"And you don't need to. Let's get in and out, and remember—"

" 'Be quiet.' "

"No, I need more than that. I need you to swear that you will stay absolutely quiet. Not a peep. No gasps, no words, nothing. Swear it."

"Kat, I don't know what the big deal is. It's just a box—"

"Swear to me," I growled. Then softening my voice, added, "Please."

"OK," he said, surprised. "I swear."

"Good. Remember when you said you wanted to help? Here's one of the crazy, batshit things we have to deal with."

I poured some powder out of a vial that I had gotten from the Other Studies Library, caking the outer rim of the box's opening so an unbroken line covered all four sides. The powder appeared as soon as it had left the invisible vial and touched the box's rim.

I looked around to see if anyone noticed what I was doing. No one seemed to take notice, so I moved onto the next, stupidly scary step.

Evil is real, and so is good. But when I use such lofty terms as "good" and "evil," I don't mean intent or even actions. I am referring to the concepts of good and evil being imbued into something. It can be a spirit or an item, or anything capable of containing an intangible concept. That is where the expressions "a good heart" and "an evil heart" come from. If you think about it, why the heart? Why not the chest or head or brain?

Well, the answer is only partly because the heart is symbolic of human emotions. The rest of the answer lies in the heart's function: to gather, hold and distribute blood. The heart is a container that constantly replenishes itself until it no longer can.

Items like vases, cauldrons and boxes can also hold good or evil … and few hold more evil than dybbuk boxes. I was about to wake up what was inside this one.

This was something that rabbis rarely talked about, but their version of an exorcism was more a trapping than an expulsion. They'd learned a way to remove a possessing demon from a human and capture it inside a container—usually a dybbuk box.

Often Jewish exorcisms would go wrong. Instead of trapping the demon in the intended box, the demon would manage to escape, only to be captured in some other container. The most famous example of this was when an unnamed rabbi trapped one in a wine cabinet that was later sold on eBay. I kid you not.

I pulled out a wig made from the ahh ... hair of a tanuki judge. This wig represented Truth and Good—capital T and G—and it was one of the purest items the Other Studies Library held.

Plucking a single strand of hair from its weave, I dropped it into the box. The effect was immediate. I felt a wave of electricity as a voice that could only belong to a demon hag crackled, "Who dares wake me?"

Several people in the room jumped in fear at the sudden noise. Then they moved on, assuming it was part of the exhibit.

The crackling voice spoke again. "I am Dybbuk, the hag of the—hold on a minute. Katrina Darling, is that you?"

14

HAGS, BOXES AND BLASTS FROM THE PAST

"*A*hh, yeah. Hi there, Ester. How's it going?"

"Oh you know, just living in a box. You could say I'm 'contained,' that I've got four walls and a roof over my incorporeal head. Say, you haven't found a way for me to get out, have you?" She stopped speaking, and I could feel her spirit trying to get out of the box. But with minimal effort, she gave up. My extra precaution—the powder, a common household salt—was unnecessary. The edges didn't even rattle. "I'm still stuck."

"Afraid so," I said.

"And you're invisible. How?"

"A potion."

"Why?"

"Oh, you know. The usual."

"The po-po on your back?"

"Yep. And where did you learn a word like 'po-po?' "

"Kevin Hart. My last owner was a big fan."

"I see."

"Good owner. Lots of entertainment. I was almost sad to make him … you know."

"Go insane."

"That's the one. But a girl's gotta do what a girl's gotta do. So to what do I owe the pleasure?"

Ester was trapped already, cursed to live in the box, and I wasn't sure what the rules for curses were anymore. I had used the salt as a precaution, an extra layer of defense, but given how quickly she'd given up trying to get out, I didn't think it was necessary.

"Your curse. I want to—"

"I don't suppose you know how to break my curse, do you?" she interrupted, her voice so excited that the box actually rattled.

"Sorry—I have no idea."

At this, she audibly groaned. "Only so much fun I can have trapped in here. Remember when you freed me the last time? Boy, did we have fun. I gave those kids a waking nightmare that had them begging you to eat them ..." Her voice trailed off as she reminisced about the good old times.

Just when I thought she was done walking down memory lane, she chirped in a tone way, way, way too jovial given the topic, "Oh! Oh, oh, do you remember when we haunted the Skirrid Mountain Inn in Wales? How many teenagers 'entering on a dare' did we get in there? First I'd drive them mad, and then you'd suck them dry. What did you used to say after every meal? The insane tasted like Cajun chicken?"

"Something like that," I said, unable to hide my shame. Justin's hand tightened on my shoulder as the dybbuk casually talked about our shared past. As much as I wanted Justin to know everything about me, my human-eating days were one thing he didn't need to know about.

"Yeah, something like that ..." Ester repeated, her own voice taking on a curious tone, like she sensed my regret. Which, given my vampiric past, was unusual.

"Ahh, Ester ... as much as I'd like to walk down evil memories lane with you, I'm on the clock here."

"Ho-hum," she replied. "So what brings you to my studio apartment?"

"A question."

Her voice became very solemn. "An exchange."

I shook my head. "No, just a question." The dybbuk's box stood silent for a minute, so I added, "Or I can leave."

"But Ka-at," Ester whined. Given her hag-like voice, it came out more like a ghost's haunting groan than a plea.

Two people walked into the exhibit room, and not wanting to be heard, I leaned in. "Ester, if I were you I would whisper lest the humans discover your presence and perform an exorcism."

I heard a low gulp before she whispered, "Kat, we're friends. Introduce me to one soul. Just like the old times. Just one soul so I may play." And therein lay the dybbuk box loophole. The box was not meant to be owned by anyone, but rather put somewhere and forgotten. If, however, the box was claimed, then the owner risked possession, and anyone the owner introduced the box to was subject to Ester's powers of possession.

I owned the box for a few years back when. Ester, evil bitch that she was, tried to possess me several times, but one of the advantages of being a vampire is that your mind is so selfish that no one, be it by magic, guile or love, can possess you.

After a few mental battles which left Ester the worse for wear, she gave up trying to enter my mind.

I guess my inner workings are too messed up even for a demon. I would be Freud's nightmare.

"No," I said, "I've come seeking an answer to one question. A question I wish you to answer honestly ... for old time's sake," I added.

"Oh come on, you don't have someone I can haunt? A person to terrorize, just a little bit? We are connected, after all. You only need to introduce me and my magic—"

"Your magic," I said. "Tell me, do you know of the limitations of magic in this new world?"

"Limitations?" she asked. "Ahh, I see what you mean. Time for magic, magic for time. I've heard that is the new world order."

"Precisely. But your curse must affect how your magic works. Have you used your magic since the gods left?"

There was a long silence before she answered. "Yes, but why do you wish to know? Katrina Darling,"—the hag paused, and I heard an audible sniff—"you smell different. No blood. You haven't fed in a long, long time."

Ignoring her, I spoke in the insistent, demanding tone I often used as a precursor to a threat. "Tell me, dybbuk demon, have you aged since the gods left?"

"Aged?"

The trouble with spirits: they don't always understand straightforward questions. And the concept of age to an immortal being was something most had yet to grasp. I tried a more archaic tact. "Does the march of time carry you in its wake and bring you closer to death with every ticking second?"

"Of course not, dearie. I am as I always was. As I always will be."

Bingo! That was all I needed to know.

"Thank you for your time, dear Ester. May time never touch you."

"And you, dearie."

Pressing against Justin's hand, I motioned for us to step back over the velvet rope.

Once across, I found his hand and put it in mine, leading him outside and away from the box.

We didn't take two steps before Justin whispered, "Phew, glad that's done."

There was a cackle that scared the three people who had wandered in so much that they literally jumped before hurrying out of the room. "Thank you, Katrina. I knew ye would nae let me down."

Looking at the box, I noted that the dividing rope was still lightly swinging from our exit. *Stupid humans and their velvet ropes.*

15

CURSES—THEY'RE NOT REAL ...
ARE THEY?

"What did I say? What was the one thing I asked you not to do?" I screamed at Justin as I led him outside and across the street.

Once we were in an alley where no one was looking, I let go of his hand. As soon as I did, I reappeared. When he saw the fire in my eyes, he said, "You told me not to say anything, but Kat ... I didn't—"

"Didn't what? Use that big mouth of yours to announce your presence to a being older than mountains and more evil than Skeletor, Azazel, Cobra Commander and just about every other evil character combined?"

"OK, OK—I messed up. But I mean, what's the big deal? It's just a voice in a box."

"Not just any voice. The dybbuk's voice. That's one incredibly evil spirit."

"Who is stuck in a box in a museum that's miles away from where we live. What's she going to do? Take an Uber and bug me?"

"You just don't get it. She is evil incarnate. She could ... she could ..."

"What, Kat? What could she do?"

The truth was, I didn't know. In the past, her magic only worked if her box was in the same room as those she terrorized. Justin was right: she was locked away in a museum in the middle of downtown. What could she do?

I would have to do research—yay, more books!—and figure it out, but just going off of what I knew about dybbuks and curses, I didn't think there was much she could do.

Still, she was ecstatic when she'd heard his voice. And spirits like her rarely tip their hand unless they think there will be no blowback, or … or unless they're messing with your head.

"I just don't know," I finally said. "Could be nothing, or she could come after you with the full brunt of her evil—"

"*ness?*"

"Yeah, that. Look, I'm not sorry I got angry, but I am sorry I put you in harm's way. I thought it would be OK, and clearly it—"

"*Was* OK. Nothing happened." He patted himself down. "See, no holes. I'm fine."

"Maybe. I … I need time to think," I said. "I'm going to walk home alone."

His eyes flickered with pain. Oh Justin, he never could hide what he was feeling. He'd be a terrible poker player.

"I'm fine. *We're* fine. I just need to think. You get that, don't you?"

He paused and nodded.

"OK, I'll see you tonight," I said as I started to walk away. "And no going back into the museum."

Justin shuddered. "Not for all the tea in China—whatever that means."

"Actually, it's an expression from—" Cutting off my own geekery, I shook my head. "I'll see you later."

And with that, I made my way back to Gardner Hall, trying to put all the pieces of the puzzle together as I did.

↔

The world is quite beautiful after a snowfall. Everything covered in white, fresh snow crunching beneath your feet. The air smells clean, as if all the smells of exhaust and dirt and people have been frozen under the blanket of newly fallen crystal fractals.

But that's only after a fresh fall. As soon as the city wakes up, starts packing the snow beneath its boots and wheels and snow plows, Montreal's dusting of serene white becomes a blanket of every shade of gray and black and guck that exists between white and black.

Since it hadn't snowed in a few days, Montreal was practically a brown paper bag that day I walked up the hill to think about my boyfriend and the hag dybbuk.

Going to the museum with him was stupid. He wasn't ready, but he was so keen to join the good fight, I thought I'd give him a taste of what the good fight really looked like.

And oh-so-smart, always-thinking-ahead me thought that "taste" should come in the form of this dybbuk—one of the oldest and most evil spirits I'd ever had the displeasure of knowing (of course, when I was a vampire, I would have substituted "displeasure" with "ecstatic joy").

With everything going on with the superheroes and their absolute lack of aging—something that shouldn't have been possible; in the GoneGod World, magic *always* costs time—I had a theory that magic might be limited, but curses might not.

The dybbuk was cursed to live in the box until the end of the world. In theory, that meant she would outlive us all. If, that was, the curse still held.

And I think it did.

My first indicator had come when the dybbuk hadn't tried to shake the salt off the edges of the box. That meant she was still stuck in there. And what was more, the fact that she hadn't aged despite using her magic meant her powers fell outside the rules of magic.

Actually, I didn't think she was using magic at all, but rather, her evil was being fueled by the curse itself. In order to understand her better, I needed to remember her curse in its entirety. Luckily for my eye-fatigued reading habit, I have a damn near photographic memory and this dybbuk's curse was something I already knew.

She was a chaos spirit, put on Earth to lead humans into evil. To—and I quote: "Infect their hearts with the desire to sin." But at the turn of the century, she was captured by a group of rabbis who confined her to a box. There she would live until this world was no more.

But despite the gods leaving, this world ticked on. It still was, so the fine print of her curse remained. She would live until this planet literally blew up.

I doubted the rabbis understood what they had done, thinking that by using the words "world no more" they would be confining her forever. But they had also granted her the power to live forever.

And so she lived in her box, only able to harm those in close proximity. There was more to her curse—much more—but for now, that was all I needed to know. The truly cursed could not die, even in the GoneGod World.

Since magic meant trading time (or life) for power, it also meant that whatever—or whoever—was causing all these superheroes to fly around and use massive amounts of power did so without fear of burning so much time that they would literally turn to dust.

And putting two and two together (something I'm so adept at doing), I needed only to find a cursed Other to figure out who was responsible for all this.

Within ten seconds of walking into Gardner Hall, I saw an acheri, a troll, a yeti, an adze and a faun. I'd have to research each and every one of their backgrounds to see if they were cursed or not.

But I also saw someone else who might offer me a clue or shortcut for figuring this out.

Underdawg.

Up, up and away.

↔

Underdawg no longer wore his red costume or cape, but instead an old t-shirt with Voltron on it, shorts and an icepack he held to his head. He was watching TV from the couch in the common room, nursing what I could only imagine was one hell of a hangover.

I walked over and plopped myself in the chair next to him. With what I hoped was an inviting smile, I said, "Remember me?"

He looked over and groaned. "Listen, if I said or did anything last night to offend you, I am so, so sorry. I'll never drink again. I swear."

"No, nothing like that. Cassy and I helped you to your room, that's all."

"Oh. Ahh ... thanks."

"Nae bother," I said. He gave me a curious look and I added, "No worries. It's Scottish for ... I'm Scottish."

And as smooth as silk, I thought—in my head.

"OK. Thanks." He turned back to the TV.

I touched his arm, a move that has gotten the attention of many an admirer. Underdawg—or rather, Boggie—didn't look at me. Either he was having the worst headache imaginable or his nerves were numbed to the point where he couldn't feel my hand.

The thought that he wasn't interested didn't cross my mind. Honest.

I squeezed his arm. "You know, last night you said some pretty crazy stuff."

"I did?" He was still looking at the TV. "Like what?"

"You said you could fly and had super strength and—" I didn't need to finish my thought because his eyes betrayed him.

He sat quiet for a long second. "I was drunk."

"Just drunk?"

"OK, drunk and a bit stoned."

"I'd say." I smiled and gave him a wink. "What happened last night?"

"Ahh, nothing. Just a wild night, that's all."

I could tell he was hiding something when he turned his body away from me. But it was more than a secret ... he was scared.

"Listen—Boggie, right?"

He nodded.

"If something is going on, you can tell me."

"Nothing's going on."

He was getting defensive, and I could tell that unless I said something he'd get up and walk away. I'd been in the confiding zone with people hundreds of times over my long, long life, and I knew enough of how this all would go down to know I had one chance to get him to open up.

If he walked away now, he'd put me into the *non*-confiding zone and never let me in. Well, not without torture.

I had to break through, and the quickest way to get someone to open up is by telling them a secret of your own.

I grabbed his hand. "And you were super strong. And dressed like Underdog." I touched his palm and whispered, "Sorry, I mean Under*dawg*, as in d-a-w-g."

I was taking a risk by admitting I had been out in the forest, but it was a risk I had to take. The superhero problem was already out of hand, and these guys still didn't know what they were truly capable of. It was only a matter of time before they started doing other, more nefarious acts that would probably involve tearing up banks, kidnapping the president's daughter or worse.

But that wasn't what I was really worried about. There were rumors that the fighting between Others and humans was getting worse. Much worse. Here in Montreal things were pretty tame—so tame that this city was a safe haven for Others and one of the few places on Earth where the multitude of species got along.

Human authorities were already blaming Others for the superhero outbreak. The last thing this world needed was an incident created by some stupid teenager with superpowers being pinned on Others and used as an excuse for further persecution of an already villainized group.

Just when I thought Boggie's eyes couldn't widen any more, they opened so wide I thought his eyeballs would fall out. "You were there."

I put a finger on the dale of my upper lip. "Shush. I won't tell if you don't."

"What's there to tell?"

"Oh, come now. How you—Boggie, a seemingly normal kid—have superpowers, for one?"

"Look who's talking."

"I don't have superpowers—I just have a mask, a dirk and a desire to throw myself in harm's way. But you … you can fly. How?"

"I … I don't know. I was hanging out with Cassy, showing her some old reruns of *Underdog*. We were laughing about how cool it would be to have superpowers and stuff and ..." He stopped, looking around.

"And?"

"You know how in *Underdog* he takes this pill to get strong and all?" he whispered. "Well, we were discussing what kind of pill I'd take to gain my powers, and we decided that it would be … you know." He made the universal gesture for toking.

"Ahh. You into the reefer, mon," I said in my best Jamaican accent.

"Huh?"

"Never mind. Go on," I said, lamenting how funny the elves found me, but how humans just didn't seem to get my sense of humor.

"So … and you've got to keep this between us."

"Hey, there are literally three people who know about my extracurricular activities—four, including you. I'm trusting you with my biggest secret, so …" I gestured for him to go on.

"So yeah," he said, nervous. "OK. Cassy—and you've got to remember we were both really stoned—she starts crying and saying something I couldn't understand. She had this really worried look on her face, like she was in pain but needed to tell me something really important.

"I tried to make her feel better—you know, comfort her."

"I'm sure you did." I winked.

"No, nothing like that." He shook his head, and then cringed in hungover pain. "I mean, Cassy is gorgeous. But she's a friend and she was really upset. The last time I saw someone so miserable was when my best friend's dad died. He cried and I knew there was nothing in the world I could do or say that would make things better. Not that I didn't try … with him, and with Cassy.

"But that was the kind of upset she was. I would never use that kind of misery to take advantage of anyone."

I could tell he was serious. Boggie, for all his own extracurricular activities, was a really good guy. "OK, sorry. I didn't mean it that way," I said. "What was she upset about?"

"I have no idea. She kept saying something over and over again, but every time I tried to catch it, it was muffled by her tears or something would happen that drowned out her words."

"What do you mean?" I said, leaning in close. "Be specific."

"I don't know," he said, thinking back to last night. "Like when she was about to tell me what upset her, my phone's alarm rang, but when I looked at it, I hadn't set it to ring. Or one time she started telling me and my coat rack broke."

"And you couldn't hear her because your coats fell?"

"It didn't just break—it shattered. Loudly." He made an exploding gesture with his hands.

"Ahh, I see," I said, not really seeing at all.

"After a while I gave up trying to figure out why she was upset and tried to comfort her. And before you make some crude joke … again, not that way. I made a joke. Something along the lines of if I was Underdog I'd carry her up, up and away, and—"

"Boggie," a voice said, out of breath, "I've been looking all over for you."

We both looked back to see Cassy walking into the common room and toward us in a huff.

And just when things were starting to make sense, I thought.

"What makes sense?" they both said in unison.

Me and my out-loudness. One day it'll get me killed.

I CAN'T HEAR YOU ... LET'S GO FOR A WALK

*C*assy sat between us, which was no small feat given I had been basically holding Boggie's hand in my *let's talk* way.

"Boggie," she said, "how are you feeling? Your head must be rattling like the bells of Pompeii when the volcano erupted."

"Interesting reference," I said, narrowing my eyes.

"We watched the movie together. You know, the one with Jon Snow in it."

"Oh, I know Jon Snow well, I do," I said in a tone a bit too creepy for my liking.

I know Jon Snow, I shuddered to myself (thankfully in my head). *What's wrong with me?*

Being around Cassy threw me off, and it wasn't just her beauty. Something else about her sent my internal compass spinning, and I didn't know what.

"So," Cassy said, "what are you two talking about? You mentioned that something made sense. What was it?"

"Ahh …" I stuttered, looking for a lie.

But before I could come up with one, Boggie sighed. "She knows."

"Does she?" Cassy said, her face draining of any hint that we were friends. I've seen that look on mountain lions just before they attacked me (and yes, that's happened to me more than once. Such is my life).

"I do." I nodded. "But I don't know why or how." The words jumped out of me and I immediately regretted them, throwing my hand up in the air like I was trying to catch them before they reached her ears.

"One more thing," Boggie said. "She's the girl in the cherub mask."

"Is she?" Cassy said. I saw her ball her hands into fists.

"Boggie!" I cried out. "That's our little secret."

"I know, I know," he said in a defensive tone. "But I can't help it." Those last words were said as a meaningless defense, as if he was merely stating the truth.

Then it hit me. He'd said it that way exactly for that reason: he really couldn't help it.

And neither could I.

"Cassy," I said, "I think we need to go for a walk."

↔

"So what are you?" she asked.

"I was about to ask you the same thing," I said, resisting the urge to blurt out exactly who and what I was. I could sense myself being compelled to answer her question, but over three hundred years of sorcerers and mages and overpowered Others wishing to use my vampiric ass for their nefarious purposes, I had built a resistance to psionic magic.

I shook my head. "Your spell won't work on me. Not now that I've become aware of it."

"Spell? I'm not casting a spell," she said, still in step with me.

I was leading her down the hill and toward campus. I might not have been able to understand who and what Cassy was, but I knew someone who would.

"Really?" I said. "You're not using a little bit of psionic magic to get me to open up?"

"No."

Her response was telling. The mere fact that she hadn't raised a curious or confused eyebrow at the words "psionic" and "magic" told me she was more than just a girl with silver hair.

"I can feel the truth desperately wanting to wiggle its way out of me and into your ears."

Cassy shrugged. "It is just my way."

"Your way? What does that mean?"

"Nothing," Cassy said, turning away and looking down the path.

"OK," I said, stepping in front of her. "Let's play a round of Twenty Questions. Only the truth. Deal?" I stuck out my hand.

Cassy looked at my hand for a long second before nodding. "Deal." But instead of shaking my hand, she grabbed my wrist.

It had been a long time since anyone had done that to me. Two hundred years and change ... but I remembered exactly what it meant. It was the old way of shaking hands between two knights or noble warriors. It meant that whatever palaver was to take place, it would be done in peace.

I grabbed her wrist back and gave it a firm shake.

↔

"Question one: How old are you?" I asked.

"Roughly three thousand, two hundred and thirty four years old," she said. "Question two: You?"

My jaw dropped, and it took me a full three seconds before I could respond. "Three hundred years and change."

"Funny how we get less and less accurate about our age as the years go on."

"Yeah," I muttered, "funny. Question three: Are you human?"

"Half," she said. "My Other side is more touch than parentage."

Touch, another ancient word. In the old days, when an Other *touched* you, they gave you a bit of their magic. It was a literal transfer of their essence into you.

She looked at me with a curious eye. "So you understand?"

I nodded.

"Then your question four should be: Who touched me?"

We both giggled. Hey, we might have been ancient beings, but that didn't mean we couldn't giggle at double entendres.

"OK, who touched you?"

"Calliope and Leigia."

"Holy shit!" I said. "A muse *and* a siren."

She nodded. "Yeah, you could say they're my fairy godparents."

"Question six: Do you still see them?"

Her gaze went distant. "Calliope, yes. But Leigia drowned when they left."

"Yeah, I heard the sirens all drowned on the day of the GrandExo-dus. But I thought that was just a rumor."

"Sadly, no." She shook her head to chase away the sad thoughts. "My turn. Question seven: Are you an Other?"

"Half-breed. But unlike you and your fairy godparents, mine was more like a creepy uncle situation."

She understood what I meant. "Were?" she asked.

"Vamp."

"Makes sense," she said. "You move too fluidly to be a were."

"Oh, how do you figure?"

"Weres are too reliant on their alternate selves. Vampires are essentially one form all the time, so they never have to practice moving in two forms. The way you dodged those guys' attacks on campus shows how practiced you are."

"Those guys—and this is my question eight—they're human?"

"Yes."

"Question nine: And you gave them superpowers?"

"Yes."

"Ten: Why?"

She sighed and looked up and down the street. It was empty—no people walking, no cars puttering along. We were basically alone, with only a couple cars buried under the snow sitting silently on the road. Then she leaned in and screamed, "Because—"

But before I could catch what she was saying the car alarms went off, ringing with obscene loudness given that they were covered in about six inches of snow.

The timing was uncanny. Beside me, all Cassy could do was shrug in response.

"I think I know what's going on here … and how to get around it. Do you trust me?" I asked, reaching out a hand.

She looked at it for a long, long time. Just when I was beginning to think she wouldn't take it, she reached out, clasping her fingers around mine.

"Thank you," I said, squeezing her hand and pulling her down the hill.

17
SOME TRUTHS GIVE YOU A STOMACH ACHE

I led Cassy to the alleyway between the bookstore and the Desautels building, where a man-looking creature whiter than snow sat on the ground reading a pile of recycled cardboard cereal boxes.

He looked pleased as he mumbled the words: "bulking agent," "polydextrose," "raising agent," "sodium hydrogen carbonate," "magnesium carbonate." He ran a sensuous finger down a box of krispies. "Mmm ... thiamin hydrochloride. Folic acid."

"Tasty?" I asked.

He nodded. "Very. FDA requirements are so ... delicious."

"I know," I said, "but do you know what's even tastier than the back of the box? What's inside."

At this he groaned and shook his head in vehement disagreement.

"Never mind all that. Cassy, meet Mergen. Mergen, meet Cassy."

"Hi," Cassy said, giving the pale creature a wave. "Aren't you cold?"

Mergen shook his head. "The truth keeps me warm."

"Speaking of truth," I said, "we wanted to see if you would hear some now."

Cassy looked at me with confusion. "I've seen a lot in my days, and yet I don't know who or what is before us."

"The Avatar of Truth and Wisdom," I said. "He eats truth. Think of him as a human lie detector, only better. And he works on Others—even touched ones."

Cassy nodded in understanding.

I'm beginning to enjoy how easy it is to speak to someone who just gets all this stuff without needing an explanation. Like sharing a kitchen with someone who knows their way around one. You never get in each other's way, you can anticipate each other's needs. It's just easy.

Not like with Justin. Cassy would have understood immediately how dangerous the dybbuk is and kept her mouth shut. And given how pretty she is ...

"Excuse me?"

I knew I should've been embarrassed at my little out loud thought, but I wasn't, merely adding (out loud on purpose this time), "Just thinking how easy it would be if you and I were a couple. You know, two ancient beings making our mark in this crazy GoneGod World."

She giggled at this. "True, but given how young you are compared to me, it would be like cradle robbing."

At this Mergen smacked his lips, evidently seeing her comment as truth.

"OK, shall we get to it? Question eleven: Are people compelled to tell the truth around you?"

"Not exactly," she said. "But they are compelled to tell me their role in ..."—she hesitated—"upcoming events."

Mergen rubbed his tummy.

"Your turn," I said.

"OK, this is my last question for you. Depending on how you answer, it's possibly the moment I walk away. Got it?"

I nodded.

"Question thirteen: Are you here to help?"

I thought about the implication of the question. She wasn't asking if I was a good guy or trying to do right. She was asking if I was here to help. Help who? Her? Others? The students? Knowing she would be particularly sensitive to my answer, I said, "I'm here to do what I believe is right. Often that means helping people. Sometimes it doesn't."

Mergen licked his fingers, and Cassy smiled.

"Did I answer well?"

"Well enough," she said. "I believe you have a pertinent question to ask. One that was so rudely interrupted before."

"I do, but before I ask that one, I've thought of a couple more. Do you mind?"

She shook her head. "Ask away. You have my trust."

"Good," I said. "Are you cursed?"

At this, Cassy's already light skin lost all color. "I cannot speak of it," she finally said.

Mergen was picking his teeth.

OK, I thought in my head. *Most people who are cursed cannot speak of what happened, or how. So that will be as close to confirmation as I can get.*

"Have you aged since they … you know … went bye-bye?"

"No," she said. "As best as I can tell, not a day."

"But you can burn time?"

"Yes."

"Did you give those students their powers?"

She nodded.

"How many?"

"As many as needed," she answered. "As of now … twenty-two."

That was an interesting answer. Twenty-two. Why that number? And what did "as many as needed" mean? Why didn't more—or fewer —need superpowers?

I really hoped my next question would shine some light on those questions as well.

"OK then," I said with a heavy sigh. Looking up and down the alley and then above, I saw nothing. Only accumulated snow on the roofs of the two building we stood between. Still, given last time's car eruption, I got myself into a position that would let me pounce at a second's notice. I also kept an eye on Mergen to see his reaction. By my estimation, a creature who ate the truth could also hear it, no matter the limitations set on it. "Let's address the elephant in the room, shall we? Tell me Cassy, why did you give those students superpowers?"

Cassy started to speak, and as she did, a sonic boom shook the ground and buildings around us. The snow slid off the roofs of the buildings, showering us in cold, white powder. And even though I couldn't hear what Cassy was saying, I knew she spoke on.

In between watermelon-sized snowfall, I saw Mergen's reaction. He gripped his belly, his eyes widening, his mouth gaping open. He looked like he was being waterboarded.

I charged at Cassy, covering her mouth. "Enough!" I said. "Enough."

Cassy was crying, her lips still moving beneath my palm. She was telling the truth—her truth. Much as I was compelled to speak mine around her, she too, was compelled to tell all of hers.

But snow and sonic booms stopped me from being able to hear her. As I tried to get her to stop speaking, I saw Mergen continuing to writhe in pain.

This lasted for an eternity. In truth she probably only spoke for ten seconds, but ten seconds was enough. When she finished speaking her truth, the snow stopped falling and the sonic booms ceased their explosive noise.

Mergen was on the floor, eyes wide open and terrified.

I went to his side. "Mergen! Mergen, are you all right?" I tried to get him into a sitting position, but he wouldn't be moved.

I was going to call for help when he grabbed the back of my head and drew me in close. "She has spoken the truth, and it is horrible."

"Mergen, will you—" But I was cut off by Underdawg dropping from the sky and landing right next to us.

Boggie wasn't wearing his mask this time. Terror had replaced it.

"The sonic booms—that was you," I said.

He nodded. "Guys, thank the GoneGods I found you. There's something horrible going on that you need to—"

But before he could finish, his youthful, unblemished face grew crows' feet. They jutted from a pair of eyes that had become white with cataracts.

His hair grayed as his cheeks sagged. He was aging. He turned from young to middle-aged to old to ancient before he collapsed on the ground.

Behind him stood a kid wearing a metal helmet not unlike a medieval knight's. On his body, chainmail and a shield with a large red cross.

"What the—?" I said, as the kid raised a hand and shot a fireball right at me.

End of Part 2

PART III
INTERMISSION

How cruel the god Apollo had been that fateful day they met. Not that she had meant to draw in the sun with her song. It was not her fault that her voice attracted the god's attention. Nor was it her fault that her beauty drove him mad with passion.

And so he came at her like a stray dog in heat, panting and begging. So distasteful. She rejected him, as was her right. Nay, more than her right—it was her nature. For when her father, King Priam, lay with her mother, Hecuba, they had enticed the muse Calliope to touch her soul and the siren Ligeia to gift her with song and beauty unmatched. And as the two divine creatures touched the newly born baby, they set her on a course to be something … more.

None could deny that Cassandra was the most beautiful girl in all of creation—even more beautiful than her sister Helen, whose face had launched a thousand ships.

But true beauty is oft accompanied by vile arrogance, and in this way Cassandra was not immune. Suitors would come from far off, lured in by Cassandra's song, only to be turned away once the hook of her perfection had pierced their hearts, its metal infecting their souls with the rabies of rejection.

On the island of Troy there is a cliff called Cassandra's Bluff, its name earned by all the failed suitors who jumped to a watery grave rather than live a life without the woman they loved with all their being.

And so that became Cassandra's curse: to love her with undeniable passion, only to find that love unfulfilled and unrequited.

Cassandra might have continued this way had her song not been heard by the sun god Apollo. Disguising himself as a human, he too sought to win her hand.

And he, like the rest of them, was refused.

But in all of creation there is no creature more vindictive than a god spurned, and refusing Cassandra's refusal, he tied her to a sacrificial altar on Mt. Olympus's Stefani Peak. There he scooped out her eyes and gouged out her tongue.

Cassandra, bloodied and in so much pain that she was near death, screamed in agony, pleading for mercy. Apollo, god of music, truth and prophesy, possessed no mercy in his pierced heart.

He replaced Cassandra's eyes with two of the all-seeing eyes of the Cyclops, so that she would be cursed with the eyes of foresight, but he made sure that the only future Cassandra could see would be the tragic death of others.

Once that was done, he sewed the vile tongue of Medacius, the spirit of fraud and deception, into her screaming mouth so that no one would believe her prophesies.

Born out of love, reborn out of pain, Cassandra awoke. She was no longer the girl gifted with beauty and song, but rather the woman who saw death and could do nothing about it for she was never to be believed.

Leaving her bleeding body, which because of Apollo's *Frankenstein*-esque tampering was no longer wholly hers, he cursed her with these final words: "Cassandra, ye shall walk this Earth never to be heard, never to help a single soul, never to die."

To be cursed with eyes not her own and magic that could not help those condemned to death—that was her punishment for denying the god Apollo the taste of her love.

If these had been the only tragedies he bestowed upon her that day, she might have found a way to accept these gifts.

But Apollo was a cruel god indeed, for he bestowed upon her one last curse, one last condition that Cassandra would find the most difficult to accept: that of life eternal.

↔

But that was then and this is now. Now Cassandra lives in a world without gods. She walks among the humans, trying to find a way to be. But being is hard, and the one thing that Cassandra hates more than anything is being ignored. It's not that she hates the feeling you get when someone is not listening—she hates *being ignored*.

It is akin to not existing, and that is exactly what happens every time she speaks. For Cassandra knows things, sees things, but every time she tries to tell someone what she sees, no one hears her.

Things are different now. Although she is still mostly unheard, she is not unseen. She has found a place among the humans (well, the normal, un-cursed humans), a place of learning, a place of enlightenment. A place that accepts those who are not quite like everyone else.

A place humans call university.

She likes her new life. She is happy to live with these youthful humans as they go about just being.

She has friends, one of whom—a boy named Bogdan, referred to by friends as Boggie—has even renamed her: Cassy. It is a good name that does not hold the burden of who she was.

Cassandra—Cassy—is the happiest she has been in as long as she can remember. But happiness is oft short-lived for most and shorter-lived for those cursed. And her prophetic eyes see death.

And not just anyone's death. It will come to so many of her friends.

She tries to warn them, but as is her curse, no one hears her.

Desperate but not entirely helpless, she has an idea. If she cannot warn them—cannot save them—then perhaps she can empower them so that they can save themselves.

18
BEHOLD, IT IS I! THE VILLAIN!
(OR ... ENTER VILLAIN, STAGE LEFT)

A fireball shot in my direction. Luckily Mergen had been reading a stack of cardboard crap that was all soaking wet from the snow. I grabbed a pile and used it as a shield. The fireball hit my makeshift shield and it went up in a burst of steam.

Shieldless and annoyed, I looked at the runt in armor. "A crusader? Seriously? Do you have any idea how much death and destruction they caused? Despite any romanticized notions you might have, let me assure you, those guys were anything but good."

I couldn't see the kid's face, so I had no idea if he was smirking or scowling. I did hear a muffled, "You talk too much," as he summoned another fireball.

So scowling, then.

The fireball grew in his hand and I had exactly two seconds to make my move. Good—two seconds was all I needed.

Most people run away from a guy with a gun. This is almost always a mistake, because running leaves you unguarded, blind and gives your enemy a nice linear target to shoot—let's say, a fireball—at.

If you're untrained, the best thing for you to do is make yourself as small a target as possible. Turn sideways, find cover—even if it doesn't cover your entire body. Standing sideways behind a four-inch-thick birch tree trunk means there's four fewer inches to hit.

The second best thing to do is to make your movements as unpredictable as possible: zigzag, slide, serpentine ... anything to make yourself difficult to track.

But if your enemy has a fireball and you're in a narrow alleyway with virtually no cover, then you only have one option.

Luckily, that one option is also your best option—if you're trained, that is ... and I had all kinds of training in me.

I somersaulted forward, and as my feet touched the ground, I used my momentum to dive into the crusader.

The result was that he dropped his half-formed fireball, which caused the snow and water around him to erupt into steam.

The crusader and I barreled out of the alleyway and onto the adjacent road. Because he was wearing heavy armor, he crashed into a snow-covered, parked car.

Peeling himself off, he left a weird, standing version of a snow angel on the car's side.

Allowing myself two seconds I didn't have, I looked over my shoulder and cried out, "Mergen, Cassy—get Boggie to safety. I'll deal with Mr. Knight Templar here."

Cassy and Mergen nodded, each throwing one of Boggie's arms over a shoulder and trotting down the alleyway.

Which left me alone with the crusader.

↔

I had a problem, and it wasn't just this LARPing nightmare trying to fry me with magic he shouldn't possess. My problem was that I was living in the modern age.

There were cameras everywhere and if I, a supposedly normal girl, did stuff I shouldn't be able to do ... that might cause some people to ask questions.

Questions like, who was I and how did I know how to do all that stuff? I might be human now, but I knew more about handling myself than any human should. And given that I wasn't ready to let the world know I was an ex-three-hundred-year-old vampire, I had to hold myself back.

That, and the small detail of this kid probably just doing whatever the cursed magic that had enchanted on him told him to do.

Still, he was different than the other heroes. He'd hurt Underdawg in a way that the superhero battle of earlier today hadn't. He had aged the poor guy to the point of near death like some sort of soul-sucking wizard, and—

Wizard Crusader, finally on his feet, swung an angry fist at me. Using my aikido training, I tried to defect the blow so it would fly harmlessly away from me and, if I was lucky (I was beginning to think I had used all my luck up), the momentum would throw him off balance.

But neither happened. Instead, when I grabbed his forearm to deflect the blow, it just kept going. I ended up flying to the side and through the window of the McGill Bookstore.

I crashed through along with a thunderstorm of McGill-branded calendars, notebooks, sweaters and t-shirts that came tumbling after me. I had just managed to get a crescent-branded flag off my face when Wizard Crusader flew through the window, landing right next to me.

"Super strength and flying ability? I could get used to this," he said, removing a glove and hoisting me up with his now naked hand. "And as for you, Katrina Darling ..."

And as he held me, I felt the strangest sensation flow over me.

It started with the tips of his fingers. I'd been hoisted off the ground by super strong creatures before. I'd felt fingertips clasp my throat. They gripped so tight that I could feel the flats of their fingers on my neck. That was what I felt at first.

Then I felt the flats open up, holes appearing where skin should be, and if that sensation wasn't enough, sharp spikes came out of them and stabbed into my neck.

Let's just say that one hurt. It hurt a lot.

He held me there for a long moment, the pincers digging deeper into my neck. After what felt like an eternity, the pincers retracted and the flats of his fingers returned. "Interesting," he said. "Perhaps that weird guy was right about you, Kat: You're not a superhero *or* an Other. You are a human girl who knows and can do more that she should be able to do."

"What 'weird guy?' " I said with gritted teeth, grabbing at his hand. My blood made his fingers too slippery for me to get a good grip.

"Some weirdo who told me some interesting things about you and your long, long past. I didn't believe him at first, but now I'm starting to." Wizard Crusader let out a long sigh. "Not that it matters. I'm not going to make the classic villain mistake. You know, reveal my plan, devise some complicated way to kill you, only to give you time to escape. I hate it when they do that, don't you?"

"I used to, but given the position I'm in, I'm kind of hoping you'll do it just this once."

He laughed, shaking his head. "In another life I would have enjoyed debating you. But alas, some things are not meant to be. How would you like to die? Broken neck? I could rip you in two. Perhaps punch a hole through your chest."

He paused and I suddenly got that his questions weren't rhetorical. He really wanted to know how I would like to die. If I had a chance to get away, it was this ... but I didn't have much time to think this through. Another second or two and he'd make the decision for me.

I thought back to what I knew about the superpowers and those pincers and in a flash of divine inspiration, I had the inkling of a plan.

A terrible plan that would probably get me killed regardless of whether I managed to escape Wizard Crusader, but a plan none-theless.

19

UP, UP AND GET AWAY?

"*I* want you to drop me."

"Excuse me?"

"Your powers, the ones you stole from Underdawg—"

"*Earned.* Not stole. I do not steal what is not mine."

"Fine," I said, rolling my eyes—a feat not easily accomplished with someone crushing your larynx. "Whatever. But if these are my last moments, I want to spend them soaring through the air."

"Interesting," he said, amused. He giggled at the thought.

"And one more thing. Because this university has caused me nothing but misery, I want you to drop me onto *The Three Bares* statue. You know what I'm talking about, right?"

"You mean that piece of concretized porn on campus? The fountain with three naked men holding a shell?"

"That's the one. I want to die plummeting into three naked guys as my final fu—"

"Language," he said, tightening his grip.

"Sorry. My final *f-you* to this place."

"Milady," he said in a mocking tone, "your wish is my command." And without another word, he took to the sky.

↔

Wizard Crusader flew out of the smashed window and up above the campus until we were hovering right above the statue. From that high, I could see it was not a shell at all, but rather a rock with a concave basin where the fountain's inner workings popped out.

Once he was above the damn statue, he flew straight up. "You know," he said, "I don't know if you'll fall straight down. Wind and all that. But I guess we must do the best we can with what we have. All of which is to say, if you miss the statue, I do apologize."

"Don't worry about it. You'll have done your best."

He chuckled. "I will have, won't I?"

"Oh yes," I yelled at the top of my lungs. "You'll do your best and I'm not going to miss. I've skydived before. I'll hit that statue if it's the last thing I do. I will destroy those damn three bares."

"Quite loud, aren't you?"

"Just psyching myself up. *I'm going to destroy that statue. I'm going to kill* The Three Bares," I sang as loud as I could.

Wizard Crusader tilted his head at me. "What are you doing?"

"Singing a song."

"A song?" he said, his voice distant.

"Yeah, a song. It's my 'Destroying *The Three Bares*' song. *I'm going to destroy that statue. I'm going to kill* The Three Bares," I sang to the tune of "Bohemian Rhapsody." "*I'm going to destroy that statue. I'm going to kill* The Three Bares."

Wizard Crusader nodded his head to my tune as he continued his ascent. Then he started singing along until the two of us were belting out *"I'm going to destroy that statue. I'm going to kill* The Three Bares" at the top of our lungs.

He kept going up as he sang, and for a moment, he seemed to have forgotten what he was doing. Then he suddenly stopped singing, instead muttering to himself, "Oh, yeah. That's right ..." before looking down and giggling to himself.

We were way up high. High enough that *The Three Bares* statue was practically a dot below.

He started giggling uncontrollably. "You know," he said between chortles, "your song was so catchy that I would have flown straight to the moon. Luckily, I got me a solid brain." He tapped the top of his helmet with his free hand. Then in a chivalrous tone, he gave me an awkward bow—given he still held me by the neck—and said, "I fear, milady, that I must bid thee adieu."

And before I could utter a word in protest, he dropped me.

↔

The only time I have ever been truly terrified as a vampire was the night a valkyrie took issue with me eating a human traveler she had taken to. Apparently, I had eaten the descendent of some great viking warrior whom the valkyrie had not only fought with, but whose family she had vowed to protect for all time.

Whoops. Silly me for not knowing that.

The avian warrior had grabbed me and taken me straight up to the sky, dropping me from a height of at least a mile.

As I fell, I'd had no idea if my vampiric body could withstand such a fall. I felt that this was truly it, and I was terrified. In the end I survived that fall, although my healing ability—which normally healed any wound in a matter of hours—took three weeks to make me whole again.

Now that I was human I knew this fall would kill me, but for some reason I was less terrified of dying. There was a part of me that knew this was how I was meant to die. Not being dropped by a maniac crusader onto a statue of three naked men, but as a human trying her darndest to make up for the shit-ton of wrong she'd done.

Dying would suck, but it wouldn't be the end of the world.

So I spread my arms and enjoyed the rush of wind on my face as the ground came closer and closer.

I gambled and lost, and somehow that's OK, I thought to myself, knowing those words to be true because I had uttered them out loud. I only ever speak the truth; my lies tend to stay in my head.

The Three Bares came rushing toward me. I had seconds left.

But as is true with all best-laid plans, sometimes they don't pay off, and sometimes they do.

There was a whoosh as a powerful hand grabbed me, and before I could say "kamehameha," I was whisked away in a golden comet of whatever is the opposite of irony.

↔

The *Dragon Ball Z*-obsessed superhero flew me to the top of the Faculty of Engineering building, where he gently put me down. "Are you OK?"

He looked right at me and, because I wasn't wearing the cherub mask, he didn't recognize me as the girl he had been trying to kill only this morning. "I am. Thank you," I said.

Comet Boy looked up at Wizard Crusader, still hovering above us, and muttered, "He tried to hurt the campus using your body."

"Ahh, I would think the more pertinent point would be, 'He tried to kill me.' "

"That, too," he said with a dismissive wave. "Whoever he is, he's going to pay." Then the kid's golden halo surged around his body as he prepared to take off again.

"Wait, wait!" I cried out. "That guy up there, with the armor—he's got weird powers. I wouldn't go up there. The last superhero he fought—"

But before I could finish my warning, the kid let out a ridiculous, anime-esque war cry and shot up into the sky.

. . .

↔

I watched helplessly as the golden comet zipped up and met the silver streaks of the crusader. The two zigzagged in the sky, Comet Boy's streaks of light linear and purposeful. Wizard Crusader, on the other hand, bobbed back and forth like a drunk trying to walk the white line.

For a moment I thought Comet Boy would take this guy down without a problem, but as he flew by Wizard Crusader, the poor excuse for a knight reached out a hand and grabbed Comet Boy.

They floated there for a long moment, hand in hand, before Comet Boy's glow fizzled out and he started to fall to the ground. Wizard Crusader's body became enflamed in gold as the other boy fell.

↔

Watching someone fall is as terrifying as falling yourself. All I could do was point and scream as the kid plummeted to the earth. I had braced myself for the ugly thud of a body hitting concrete when a girl dressed in black leapt into the sky and caught the boy, gently bringing him down to the ground.

I looked down from my perch on the engineering building's roof and spotted several more heroes showing up. They were all staring up at Wizard Crusader with growing anger.

For a second I thought there would be an epic showdown, but Wizard Crusader did the smart thing: he took off, leaving a golden streak in his wake.

20
THE GERIATRIC WARD OF HEROES

I kicked in the locked rooftop door and made my way down the stairs to where the heroes were gathering. They all stood around Comet Boy, who lay there as human as the day he was born. Well, that's not quite right. He was old, and I don't mean *grand-father* old. I mean forgotten-in-a-home old.

Liver spots, wrinkles, moles and skin tags plagued his face. His nose had grown three times larger and was covered in deep holes … a whisky nose, as we'd say in Scotland. Seemed that Comet Boy, if he had had a chance to grow old, would have done so with a wee bit of an affinity for drinking.

The girl in all black gently hoisted the old man up so that his head lay on her lap. "Dustin? Dustin—what happened?" she said between confused tears.

"I … I don't know—" Dustin started to say, but when he heard his own voice, he paused. "Why do I sound like that?"

A dozen superheroes all stared down at him, not one of them wanting to tell him. He looked at his girlfriend. "Mary, what … what's wrong with me?"

"I … I don't know how to tell you." She started to pull out her phone, presumably to show him what happened. At least I hoped that was her purpose and not to take a selfie for Instagram.

I pushed my way through the crowd and bent down next to him. Grabbing Mary's phone out of her hand, I shook my head. "We need to do this right," I said.

Twenty minutes ago he'd been eighteen, maybe nineteen. Now he was older than sin, which meant his heart was ancient as well. The shock could kill him.

Holding the phone with two hands, I said, "First of all … Anton, is it?"

He nodded.

"I want you to know this is reversible. There are ahh … treatments that can be done and magic that can be used."

"Magic?" he asked.

"Yeah, magic."

"Why do I need magic to fix my voice?"

"Because," I said, clicking the phone's camera function on, "something unusual has happened to you. Something terrible. But—and I can't emphasize this enough—it is *reversible*. Remember that." I handed him the phone.

He looked at himself and pulled the phone away. "Oh, ha ha. This is some new app effect, right?"

His eyes darted between Mary and me, and when he saw that neither of us were smiling, he groaned "Oh Jesus, I'm too young to be old," before fainting.

↔

We didn't know what to do. The old-young guy (young-old guy?) was out cold, and for all we knew, heading toward the light.

We called an ambulance, which swiftly arrived and picked him up. There was a brief discussion about his name and stuff, and given that they would never believe his ID belonged to this old guy, we said he had none. They took him without a second question.

Thank the GoneGods for Canada and their universal healthcare.

↔

I went to the alleyway, hoping to find Cassy, Boggie and Mergen—or at the very least, Mergen—but none of them were there. Instead, there was a cardboard sign with three words on it: *Royal Vic, Bogdan.*

The Royal Vic was the hospital that was so close to McGill's residences that Gardner Hall practically shared a backyard with the place. Evidently Cassy had the same idea of getting her old guy to the hospital as well.

I trudged up the hill and made my way to the hospital lobby where Mergen sat outside, still groaning and clasping his stomach.

I have only ever seen Mergen groan in discomfort when he was forced to digest some particularly terrible lie. That he was still hurting meant that whatever Cassy had told him was practically food poisoning for the poor guy. "Did she lie to you?" I asked, but I already knew the answer. There was far too much meat on his bones for him to have been lied to.

Mergen shook his head. "No. Her truth is not meant to be heard."

"She's cursed?"

He cupped both his hands together and mimicked eating heartily out of them.

"So, *big time* cursed?"

He nodded again.

"And whatever she has to tell us—about the superheroes and what she's up to—you can't hear it, either."

Mergen paused and shook his head. "Heard it."

My eyes widened in surprise. "You heard it? Then what is it?"

"I cannot say."

"Why not?!" I yelled, then realizing where I was, caught myself and counted to ten before saying in a far more civil tone, "Why not?"

"Because … " He gestured vomiting and then stuff coming out of the other side, before placing a hand over his stomach and mimicking a scene from *Aliens*.

"It will kill you, eh?"

"Not just kill. Devastate."

I imagined the scene out of *Monty Python* where the fat man ate so much he literally exploded, and I looked at my friend with sorrow. As much as I wanted to know Cassy's secret, I wanted to know that my friend was safe and healthy. Taking his hand in mine, I said, "Then never tell. Not one word to anyone. Ever."

He nodded.

"They're inside. I should go."

I pulled away but Mergen held onto my hands. "What?" I asked. "Is there anything you need?"

Letting go, he pointed to his stomach and groaned. "The truth."

Mergen was in pain and needed a bit of truth to offset whatever Cassy had done to him.

"OK," I said. "You want some truth? Here you go. When I get to the bottom of this, someone is going to pay—dearly."

"Mmm, yes," Mergen said. "Such lovely truth."

↔

"Ahh, hi," I said to the nurse at the help desk. "I'm looking for my grandfather … Bogdan. He came in a bit earlier. You might remember him—he was dressed in a red superhero costume, complete with a cape and all." I made like I was Superman (or, in my case, Super-woman) flying through the sky in an attempt to lighten the mood.

The nurse didn't smile. "What's going on today? Your grandfather is the fourth elderly man dressed up as a superhero to come in."

I had feared this but wasn't entirely surprised. Wizard Crusader's powers were too eclectic and I figured he had stolen a few super-heroes' powers. Now I had confirmation that he had stolen at least four.

"Comic-Con … with an emphasis on superheroes of the past."

"I hope they sell insurance with their entry tickets," she said, laughing at her own joke. (Which was disappointing … mine was funnier.)

Now it was my turn not to laugh. The nurse tapped on her computer. "Third floor—room 319."

With a "Thank you," I made my way to Boggie, only to find the kid wizard, Spider Guy and Cheetara prone on their own hospital beds, still wearing their costumes which were now far too big on their brittle frames.

Someone's going to pay. And pay very dearly indeed.

21

SORRYS, SIRENS AND SONGS

*H*ave you ever truly explored the ravages of age? I don't mean looking into your grandfather's eyes or running your fingers along your grandmother's wrinkles. And I certainly don't mean discussing with some friend or relative about how time has caught up with them and whether they need more help now.

Old age is terrifying. As in soul-crushingly, knee-wobblingly, nightmare-inducingly terrifying. And everything horrible about it stems from one undeniable and sad fact: as your body grows weak, your mind grows stronger. I believe it is this contrast that makes mortality truly cruel.

Seeing Bogdan sleeping there, his body devastated by time he hadn't spent, I couldn't help but examine every liver spot, every wrinkle, every tiny imperfection now graffitied across his face. And the prevailing thought running through my head wasn't about the injustice that had been done to poor Underdawg. No, my first thought was this shameful one: *Thank the GoneGods it wasn't me.*

I'm ashamed that was my first thought on seeing him lying helpless on that hospital bed. But as ashamed as I was, my second thought was no better: *That will be me one day.*

That thought set my head to spinning ... and made me wish I was a vampire again. Not the first time I'd wished that since becoming mortal, but it was probably the one time I would have happily accepted the vampiric virus in my body for a second chance at immortality.

I guess it makes sense I'd feel that. After all, I didn't age a day for three hundred years. Hell, I didn't age a second. I was frozen in time, cursed to be forever young. And, in the dead of night when I cannot deny what I truly feel, I loved it. I loved being a vampire. The power, the confidence, the knowledge that no matter what happened, I was strong enough, fast enough, smart enough to deal with it.

Such a contrast to being human.

And even though I'd only aged four years since the gods left, from the beginning I became particularly sensitive to the tiny aches and breaks that my body started experiencing. I felt them all because, as minor as they were, my body hadn't felt anything like that for centuries. Those minor indications of time marching on in both my body and soul stood out like signposts in an otherwise empty desert.

And every time I felt one, I would freeze in anguish and self-pity as the thought *"I'm going to die one day"* rang in my mind.

That was exactly what I felt the afternoon I saw Boggie lying there. *I'm going to die. Maybe not today or tomorrow, but one day I'm going to die. And not just me ... we all are. The day the gods left, every single one of us were cursed to die.*

"I wish," Cassy said, her words bringing me back to reality as her eyes admonished me for thoughts that should have been private but had instead been uttered out loud. "Come, pay your respects. He's in this state because instead of running away, he came to warn us. For that we owe him our thanks."

I nodded. "Sorry."

Cassy huffed. "No, it is I who am sorry. I shouldn't be so cruel. Existential crisis aside, we also owe *you* thanks. Your bravery saved us all."

I did what I always do when praised: I curtsied. It was an old habit ingrained in me as a child and despite the passage of hundreds of years, I still did it.

I guess time can't kill everything.

Walking over to Boggie, I took his frail hand in mine and gave it a gentle squeeze. Even though my touch was light, almost imperceptible, he woke.

"Hey—it's you. Angel Girl."

"It's Kat, Boggie. From earlier."

"I know. I'm old, not senile. Angel Girl's your superhero name. You know, because of …" he lifted his hand to his face.

"Got it," I giggled. "But I prefer Cherub."

"Ohh," he rasped. "That's way better than Angel Girl. OK Cherub, what's the rub?"

Now I positively chortled. I saw why Cassy liked him; despite nearly being killed and aged beyond his years, he still managed a smile. A rare quality these days. "The rub," I said, "is that the villain is still at large, still stealing life and superpowers and still an asshole."

"Amen," Boggie said.

"But we're going to get him. We can't take him on head-to-head—he's too powerful—but perhaps a trap, or maybe someone could reverse the spell and take him down a notch. Ahem, ahem." I pointed at Cassy.

The impossibly beautiful girl with silver hair shook her head. "I can't."

"Why not?" Boggie asked. "I don't need to be Underdawg anymore." He gestured to the other aged superheroes in the room. "None of us need to be super anymore."

"I know," Cassy said, her voice quivering. "I know." She stood up in frustration and walked to the window. Placing two hands on the window pane, she groaned. "But that's not how my magic works. I didn't cast a spell … I cursed you."

"Oh," I said, understanding dawning within me.

" 'Oh' what?" Boggie tried to sit up, but he wasn't used to being old and sat up too fast. He lay back down with a yelp of pain, a shaking hand at the small of his back.

I came to his side and helped him down, then I handed him the remote to his bed. "Use this."

He pushed the button that placed him in a sitting position. As the machine hummed and Boggie slowly folded into an upright position, he repeated his question. " 'Oh' what?"

"Curses aren't like spells," I said. "You can't turn them off or do something that reverses the effect. The only way to stop a curse is to break it."

"So break it."

"She can't. Can you?" I looked up at Cassy.

Cassy didn't turn from the window, simply shaking her head as her hand continued to press against the pane.

"I can't break the curse—but you can," she said, not looking at either of us.

"How?"

"By fulfilling your purpose."

↔

"OK," Boggie said, getting more and more excited. "I'll do it. Just tell me what I have to do." He pointed at me like I had the answer.

"Hey, don't look at me—I have no idea how to break your curse. Cassy does."

Cassy didn't say or do anything, just continued to stare out the window.

"Cassy," Boggie said, "tell us. How can we break the curse?"

Cassy didn't respond for a long time, and I was beginning to think she wouldn't tell us how to break the curse. That, or she couldn't. Then she sighed and, being very careful, she said, "There is a place where Death comes flying from above. She is the anger of the unentitled. She is the fury of the mistreated. She wears the mask of the righteous, though she is anything but, for her anger and fury is misplaced. Stop her. Convince her she is wrong, and your curse will be lifted."

"What the hell does that mean?" Boggie said.

I shook my head and stood. I crossed the room and put a hand on Cassy's shoulder. "It's a prophecy. They're meant to be cryptic because … well … prophets are often cursed so that people will not hear them. Cassy here is doing her best to warn us in such a way that we can both hear her and have a chance to do something about it. She's told us everything she can."

Pulling her from the window, I turned her around and looked her in the eyes. "Isn't that right, Cassandra, Prophetess of Doom?"

Cassy turned, her wide eyes all the confirmation I needed.

"It took me a while to figure it out," I said. "It's been years since I studied the classics—but that's you, isn't it?"

Cassy answered with eyes that welled up with tears. So that was one mystery solved. We weren't dealing with just any cursed person— we were dealing with the *original* cursed human.

And on hearing her name, Cassandra, sister of Helen, daughter of King Priam of Troy and cursed Prophetess of Doom, wept.

↔

Cassy wept for several minutes before gathering herself. Looking over at Boggie, who stared up at us with confusion painted on his face, she said, "I was cursed by the god Apollo to see death and be powerless to stop it."

That was the thing about curses. They compel you to action—and not just any action, but the most straightforward, simplest route to accomplishing whatever you've been cursed to do.

And seeing Cassandra … Cassy … I understood her burden. She was cursed to both see the future and have no one believe her. You'd think after a few hundred years of prophesizing doom and gloom, she'd give up. Or at the very least, she'd become desensitized to people's suffering.

But seeing her cry before me showed the opposite. She cared.

She cared just as she had cared during a thousand tragedies before this one and would care for a thousand more.

She cared partly because of who she was, but mostly because she was compelled to do so.

That is the nature of a curse: you are almost forced to act in ways that are in direct conflict with your desires. That's the cornerstone of your curse.

That is why the students had been attacking each other. It had started with the Jessica Jones look-alike throwing a truck at her boyfriend. In other words, she'd been damaging the campus—the very thing the superheroes were cursed to protect.

But when a rhino pummels you, there's bound to be collateral damage ... damage which summoned more heroes, who in turn did more damage, and so the cycle continued—and might have continued for who knew how long—until I did something *dramatic*.

Springing the leak in the water main was just dramatic enough to get their attention and draw them away from the very place they were meant to protect.

↔

"Cursed, huh?" Boggie not so much asked as muttered to himself. I could recognize his mortal mind wrestling with what was happening. I'd seen Justin struggling in the same way quite a few times.

Cassy nodded. "More than cursed. What Apollo did to me was a malediction." Her voice took on a woeful quality. " 'Cassandra, ye shall walk this Earth, never to be heard, never to help a single soul, never to die.' "

We were all silent until Boggie broke the hush with, "Damn, that is one cold dude."

Cassy and I looked at the aged teenager, who returned our indignant gazes with a huge, gaping smile. "Well, it's true."

That was too much. After hearing those last words, the three of us burst into laughter. Hard, long, wonderful laughter. Gallows humor— the best remedy when overcome by sadness or tragedy. I had known many people in my life, more than most, and few could truly be funny in moments like these, often choosing self-pity or fear over a joke.

Boggie didn't wallow in either. He chose to laugh as he marched to his death, and I liked him all the more for it.

Cassy went over to Boggie and ran her fingers along his hair. "You could always make me laugh, Boggie. That's why, when I saw your death, I knew I had to do something. And then I thought, 'I may not be able to warn you or save you, but I might be able to give you the power to save yourself.' That's why I gave you superpowers. So you would have the power to save yourself. I did all this. I tried and I failed. I am sorry. I am so, so sorry."

Cassy started to cry again. Boggie, weak as he was, pulled her in for a hug. "Shuush, shuush … you did your best."

"But I didn't save you. I hurt you, and not just you. The others, too."

"You did, but as my mother always said, 'Accidents happen and we can only do our best.' Of course, she'd say that with a ladle in hand as she prepared to spank my brother and me for breaking a vase or something." Boggie giggled, and so did Cassy.

They sat together for a long moment, not speaking, just being together before Boggie, being Boggie, said, "So you're the Prophetess of Doom, eh? I don't know if anyone's ever told you this before, but that's one kickass superhero name."

↔

"So now what?" Boggie asked.

"Now we try to figure out what the curse is about and save the day. That would be difficult enough, but one of the people you're trying to save has turned out to be a homicidal maniac."

"No problem, Cherub," Boggie said. "You kicked his ass once. You can do it again."

"I didn't kick his ass. Believe me—I barely escaped with my life."

"But you did," Cassy said.

"Actually, it was this guy who saved me."

"Boggie?" Cassy asked.

"Yeah," I said, taking Underdawg's aged hand in mine. "I remembered what you told me about your powers and how they were activated by … you know …" I held a forefinger and thumb to my lips.

Boggie did the same with a giggle.

"So I figured a crusader—a holier-than-thou type—would never partake in the stuff. I also figured that Underdawg's powers and the more enlightened state of mind one achieves when high go hand in hand. That was my gamble, and I was right.

"The higher we went, the more he giggled and sang along to my stupid song. And I needed to buy myself as much time as I could, because—"

"You needed the other heroes to show up," Cassy said.

"Exactly. That was my second gamble: that they would turn up to protect the campus. And just when I was about to do a swan dive into *The Three Bares* … well, that's when he showed up." I pointed at Comet Boy, who lay asleep on his hospital bed.

"Yes," Cassy said, nodding, "very wise. When I designed the curse, I did so because I needed—"

But before she could say anything else, Boggie and Comet Boy's EKGs flatlined with that screech of death. For a moment I thought the two were actually suffering from cardiac arrest, but neither clutched his chest or showed any pain. Boggie's face just showed confusion.

It seemed Cassy still couldn't tell everything she needed to.

Two nurses ran into the room, sighing in relief when they, too, realized it was a machine malfunction. Resetting the machines, the elder of the two pointed at her watch. "Five more minutes, guys. Your grandfather needs to rest."

I winced at the word "grandfather," and Cassy let loose a tear down her perfect cheek.

Boggie, on the other hand, chuckled. " 'Grandfather.' Never thought I'd live long enough for anyone to call me that."

↔

We left Boggie to his hospital bed and cable television, leaving the hospital in silence. As we did I mulled over what was going on. Cassy gave those kids superpowers to protect them from some great evil that was coming after them. Whatever was coming was going to kill them and Cassy did the only thing she could think of to save them. She gave them superpowers.

We went outside where I turned to Cassy and said, "We have to warn them. The superheroes ... we have to tell them something is coming after them."

"I can't," she said. "I would if I could. Hell, I wouldn't have—"

"Maybe you can't, but I can ... I know I don't know the specifics, but I know enough to give them a heads up, a fighting chance. I suspect their deaths will come at the hands of the Crusader."

I let my thought hang there to see if Cassy would ... could ... give me a sign to see if I was right.

Cassy said nothing.

"Fine ... regardless of whether or not the Crusader is the big bad, we need to at least tell them about his ability to steal powers. They'll need them for whatever is coming."

Cassy nodded in understanding and then in agreement.

"I don't suppose you have a list?"

Cassy shook her head. "No, but I have a song."

22

PRESIDENTIAL FIGHTS AREN'T VERY PRESIDENTIAL

*L*eaving Cassy and Boggie and the other aged superheroes in the ward, I made my way home. I had a lot to plan and not much time to get it done. All we needed now was for a superhero skirmish to break out and Wizard Crusader to suck up all their powers in one go.

Time is of the essence, I thought (probably out loud, but since I was alone, I had no idea) and then cringed at the cliché. You'd think the inner workings of my mind would be wittier. Guess not.

But time *was* of the essence. We had the superhero problem, the aging issue and lifting the curse. Then there was that weird thing Wizard Crusader had said in the bookstore. *"He told me about you."*

Who was "he?" And what did Wizard Crusader know about me? That I was the Cherub or an ex-vampire? That I often wore platform shoes to appear taller or that even though I was a natural redhead, not *this* shade of redhead?

What?

I needed to figure that out as well. I'd amassed many enemies in my lifetime, and if one of them was rearing their ugly head, it meant—beyond the issue of twenty-two superheroes trying to squash me like a bug—another player was out to get me.

The trouble with out-to-get-you type players ... they often use your friends as leverage. If Justin got kidnapped one more time because of me, I was sure he'd dump me.

I shook my head, trying to break loose the myriad of problems swimming in my head. I figured I had a few phone calls to make, some plans to sort out, then I'd have a few hours—the calm before the superhero monsoon—in which to watch a movie and chill. Since I was in an epically bad mood, I needed something to lift me out of it.

And I knew just the remedy: *Legally Blonde 1* and *2*.

I was climbing the final stairs up to Gardner where a very impatient and frustrated Andrew stood waiting for me. As soon as I made it to the landing, he lifted his phone. "What is the point of having one of these if you're never going to answer it?"

"What are you—?"

"I must have called you a hundred times. We have a debate. Well, had a debate. In the end, it was just Harold, some fool named Michael who kept talking about beer and a girl named Aimee who spoke so softly we could barely hear her."

"Aimee? Mousy girl. Kind of cute. Real shy," I said, pushing my way past him. "I know her from—" I stopped myself. The truth was, I knew her because she had been friends with a gargoyle I'd also known who was killed during my first day on campus. Long, sad story. "I had no idea she was running. Good for her."

" 'Good for her?' Good for her!" Andrew cried out. "Give me a break. Do you know what essentially happened? An idiot, a shy girl and a bigot. And the voice of reason, our heroine—who in this scenario is you—wasn't there. Do you know what people are saying about you?"

"Not a clue," I said, unlocking Gardner Hall's front door.

"You haven't been checking Twitter."

"I don't have Twitter."

"A presidential candidate without Twitter?" he said in an exasperated voice. "Well, I do. And here's what they're saying: 'Kat Darling too scared to debate.' 'Another pretty girl who thinks she can get by on her looks alone.' "

"Ahh, they think I'm pretty."

"That's not the point—"

"I get the point. I'm being judged one tweet at a time. Message received."

"And?"

"And what?" We stood in the foyer of Gardner Hall. My room was one floor below. His five above. And yet here we were, fighting on ground zero.

"And where were you?" He crossed his arms as he waited for my answer.

I was exhausted and had a million things to do. As much as kicking Harold's ass was something I would relish doing, I had bigger events than worrying about a rez election. But Andrew deserved an answer. Or at the very least, an apology.

That would be the mature thing to do.

But as always, Katrina Darling, a.k.a. The Ex-Vampire, a.k.a. The Girl Trying To Be Human Again, a.k.a. The Cherub, came rushing to the fore to do what she always did ... she made things worse.

"I was getting my nails done." I held up my hands to show him ten very *not* done nails.

"Oh, ha-ha," he said. He took a deep breath. "Look, we can still get ahead of this thing. We have to release a statement telling everyone you were somewhere else ... somewhere more important. That's why I want to know where you were. Maybe we can use that. If not, we can always—"

"I wasn't anywhere. I forgot," I lied. The sad thing about this whole fight was that I *was* somewhere more important. And even though I couldn't mention the fight or Wizard Crusader, I could say I was in a hospital visiting a friend.

The truth. It will set you free.

More clichés and more truth I wasn't going to share with Andrew or anyone else. I might have had a good excuse, but if I was honest with him, I would say that I didn't have time to do my own home-work, let alone run for Gardner Hall's president.

But instead I looked into his hurt, disappointed eyes and said,

"Look, I don't know what you expected from me. I don't know who you thought I was—"

"I thought you were different," he said in a curt tone. Except to call his tone curt would be like saying a lion "meows." It just doesn't do it justice. It was as if a switch had been turned off in his mind and I, the switch's recipient, went from being someone in Andrew's life to being dead to him.

No, worse than dead—it was as if he erased me from himself.

That feeling was eerie, annoying and enraged me even more. "Well, I'm not. I'm just like everyone else: selfish, entitled and not about to waste my time on anything I don't believe in."

"I see that now," he said with a voice so robotic and devoid of emotion, it would make the Terminator proud.

"Good," I said back. "Because the sooner you and everyone else sees it, the sooner I'll be left alone."

I walked to the stairwell and started down to the basement.

"You know," Andrew said coolly after me, "we could have made a difference, you and I."

"Maybe," I said with an exhausted sigh. "The trouble with making a difference is that different isn't always better."

And with that, I continued my descent.

23

PLANS, LEGALLY BLONDES, SLEEP AND REVERSIONS

I knew I should have felt bad about letting Andrew down, but I didn't. There was something about the way he'd switched from being my friend to a venomous snake.

Don't get me wrong—I deserved it. But when most people are let down, they argue, plead, storm off ... and then you find an angry letter in your inbox or slipped under your door. That's followed by the cold shoulder.

Andrew wasn't like that. He just went cold. Like as soon as I let him down, I became a non-entity in his mind. Weird, but it did give me a wee bit of insight as to why Cassy didn't like him. Someone who can turn on a dime like that tends to be the kind of person you avoid.

Whatever his problem was, I couldn't worry about that now. I picked up my phone and thought about who to call. Egya and Deirdre, of course, but there was someone else that could prove more useful than either of them.

Someone who had experience organizing things.

Someone who knew how to mobilize and motivate large groups of people in a short period of time.

I dialed the number and he answered on the first ring. "Hey there, lover," I said. "Remember when you said you wanted to be part of the team? Well, I have just the job for you."

"Hell yeah," Justin said, and I could only imagine him lifting an incredibly sexy arm in triumph.

↔

After I'd worked through the particulars with Justin, I called Egya and laid out the plan to him as well. The Ghanaian cackled as I told him what the stakes were and how we were going to deal with them.

After hearing his role in the whole thing, he didn't just cackle. He guffawed. For a full minute.

You know what it's like to be on the phone listening to someone laugh uncontrollably? I did now, and it was something I could have lived another three hundred years happily never knowing.

↔

With the plans set, all I had left to do was wait. Good—I'd planned for that, too. I needed a distraction from the superheroes, from the guy lurking in the shadows, from my crazy life in general.

There was so much I had no control over and only so much I could take. I was only human, after all. If I were a vampire again, all of this would have been so much easier to handle. But I wasn't, so I focused on what I did have control over … *Legally Blonde*. I turned on the movie for the umpteenth time and just about made it to the point where Warner Huntington III breaks up with Ella before I fell into a deep sleep.

I guess fighting superheroes all day takes it out of you.

That afternoon I dreamt ... but it wasn't just a dream. It was a memory with a very strange twist.

After a long day of battling superheroes and dealing with prophetesses of doom, I wandered into the Other Studies Library to ... well, I don't know why I went. Dreams rarely make sense. All I knew was that I needed to be in the library.

I wandered to the back area where the public part of the library's museum was housed. There, I found the display cases normally filled with artifacts donated by Others, sorcerers and witches completely empty.

Panic grew in me as I rushed between the cases, looking for some evidence of where the goods were and who could have stolen them. Some of these items were quite powerful, and in the wrong hands could do a lot of harm.

But there was no evidence of a break-in, no indication that the locks were forced. The artifacts were just gone.

The library had security cameras, I thought. *Perhaps they had some footage—*

"Still talking out loud, Peculiar Girl," said an old and familiar voice.

I turned to see a very old man dressed in a tweed blazer, giving me a knowing look.

"Dr. Dewey—"

"Ah, ah, ah." He raised a scolding finger. "I thought we had a deal. No names, remember?"

"Yes," I said, fighting against the growing lump in my throat. "I remember, Old Librarian. No names."

"Good," he said, smiling as I called him by his name.

"You're dead," I said.

"I am."

"And this is a dream?"

"I suppose so, but this is a dream that can only happen because of two very important reasons. Care to guess what they are, Peculiar Girl?"

"Not another riddle. I've had just about as much of riddles and prophesies that I can stand and—"

"Indulge an old man, will you?" he said with very serious, caring eyes. It had been months since I'd seen this man alive and even though I had hardly known him, he had been the first friend I'd made at university. I hadn't realized it—or probably more accurately, I hadn't allowed myself to realize it—but I missed the Old Librarian. Very much.

"OK," I said. "Anything for an old friend. What are the clues?"

"I already gave them to you," he said, gesturing to the room. "You have everything I can tell you."

"All right," I said, drawing out the word. I knew this was a dream and I truly did hate riddles, but somehow I felt compelled to play his game.

"*Compelled*," I thought. *That's an interesting way to have phrased it.*

I tried to recall everything I knew about dreams. For one, everything came from you, so if I had used the word "compel," that meant something.

And given everything going on—the curses and everyone being compelled to do things they wouldn't normally do—it could be because I'm cursed, too.

"You are so smart," the Old Librarian said. "So, so smart."

"But I'm not a superhero."

"No, you are something else. And you are not cursed the way you will think you are. Remember that."

"I am not cursed the way I *will* think I am ... as in future tense?"

"Indeed," he said, nodding as a sadness crept into his eyes. "There are forces at play that are playing you. Using you. Tread carefully, Peculiar Girl."

"Forces? What kinds of forces?"

"Some will say Destiny, others Fate. I say that these are lofty terms used by little people who understand neither Destiny nor Fate. The universe is vast and full of mystery—even more so now that the gods are gone, for we can no longer point to them as explanations for all that we do not understand."

"And what are you? The anthropomorphization of my subconscious, warning me about something that my conscious mind doesn't quite see?"

The Old Librarian laughed and wagged a finger. "So smart. Perhaps too smart for your own good. No, I am not your subconscious. I am, in as real a way as possible given that I'm dead, the Old Librarian."

"So you're real? I mean, real even though this is a dream?"

"I am as real as the confines and rules of this universe allow me to be."

"Because that clears things up," I said, not hiding my sarcasm.

He chuckled and took off his tweed jacket so he could undo the top two buttons of his shirt.

"This isn't going to turn into one of those kinds of dreams? Because if so, show me the exit."

"You are so smart, Peculiar Girl, but sadly, not so witty." He took off his glasses in a very purposeful way, folded them and set them on one of the empty display cases. "I have one more clue I can give you before I go. Not so much a clue, I suppose, but rather a question that you must ask yourself in order to understand why and how I sought you out this day."

"OK," I said, goosebumps running down my spine. *This is just a dream,* I tried to reassure myself, but reassurance would not come. Only dread and fear.

"Ask yourself, Peculiar Girl, now that the gods are gone ... where do souls go after the body dies?"

"I ... I don't know."

"No one does," he said. "That doesn't make the question any less important. Now, do what you must." He pulled at his shirt collar as he stretched out his neck, inviting me to ... what? Bite him?

I was human. I no longer bit anyone (well, sometime Justin in jest, but that was it), and yet seeing the large jugular vein exposed on his aged neck, I felt drawn to him.

And the life force flowing within him.

Compelled in that nonsensical way only true of dreams, I came forward, wrapping my arms around him. I placed my lips on his neck, and expecting him to draw away, I held him tighter. But he didn't try to pull away.

Instead, he stayed perfectly still.

I hesitated, and the Old Librarian said, "Peculiar Girl, do as is your nature."

My nature? I was human, but if I were a vampire, my nature would have been to ... bite.

I bit down hard on his neck, positioning my fangs to pierce his jugular vein. The blood erupted out of him. Warm and glorious and comforting and—

Holy shit, I'm killing him, I thought, pulling away from him and from my dream.

I woke up in a near scream. Thank the GoneGods it was just a dream.

↔

I woke up desperate to get the taste of blood out of my mouth. Dream or not, that felt way too real, and the memory of how glorious blood tasted when you were a vampire came flooding back to me. Also, killing the Old Librarian—someone I had considered a friend—was terrifying.

And what was up with all the riddling stuff? I knew it was just a dream, but I also knew enough about dreams to realize that sometimes they shouldn't be dismissed. I'd have to mull over the Old Librarian's words, but later. Now I needed to get ready for tonight's festivities.

When I got up, I found Deirdre meditating naked in the middle of the floor. And given she was in the lotus potion, she looked damn good. Then again, Deirdre was blessed with such a perfect body that she'd look good picking her toenails naked.

Moving as quietly as I could so as to not disturb her, I made my way to the other side. Something was off and my first thought was that the room was pitch black. But it was nighttime and we were in the basement, so darkness wasn't unexpected. What *was* strange was how well-adjusted my eyes were. I could see everything—including Deirdre's lotus-ness—so well that I thought she must have left the lights on …

But they were off.

OK, light streaming from beneath the door? I looked at the threshold, expecting to see an overbearing glow entering my room, but instead I saw the usual amount of neon.

Whatever, I thought. *Still got my spaghetti brain on. A shower will wake me up.*

I grabbed my toiletries and walked into the bathroom. Showered, did a couple unmentionables, and it was time to brush my teeth.

Shoving my toothbrush into my mouth, I considered all I had to do today. The gathering would start in a couple hours and—

As I brushed, I felt two familiar bumps in my mouth.

Very familiar.

Parting my lips wide, I looked into the mirror and saw—

"No, no, no!" I cried out.

Deirdre was in the bathroom in a flash. "What is it, milady?" she said, before narrowing her eyes in confusion. "Milady, you have fangs."

24
REGRESSION IS A BITCH

*D*eirdre reached out to me with one hand while balling the other into a fist. I understood the conflict in her being immediately. The fae saw vampires as abominations created by dark magic. Fae, being fae, did not dabble in dark magic. Ever.

But their sworn enemies and counterparts—orcs, goblins and trolls—did, and Deirdre, being a fae changeling warrior, was sworn to fight those forces of evil until her dying breath.

And here I was ... a vampire. Something that could only happen because of dark magic.

But I was her friend, too. The girl who she'd sworn her sword arm to on the first day of school and someone with whom she'd fought side by side in numerous situations.

I was a vampire and she didn't know what to do.

Well, that made two of us. I touched one of my fangs, pressing my thumb into its point and drawing blood. I looked at my thumb, which immediately healed. How vampire-y of me.

"What ... what happened, milady?"

"If I knew, I would tell you," I said, flexing my muscles as I felt familiar strength flowing through my veins.

I was starting to feel old urges. Hunger for blood was one, but that wasn't the worst urge surging through me.

An old selfishness crept into my being. A feeling that I was no longer concerned with mortals and their little ways ... that I was something more—something else.

"No," I said, chasing that sense of superiority away, "this is just the curse. Before sleeping I thought to myself that all this would be easier if I was a vampire again. What is the human expression? 'Be careful what you wish for.'"

I stopped talking, mulling over my choice of words: *"What is the human expression?" "Human expression?"* It wasn't taking long for me to revert to old habits.

I slammed my hand onto the porcelain sink, shattering it. Shit ... how was I going to explain that to the residential admin? "Sorry, but now that I'm a vampire again I simply don't know my own strength."

I'd worry about that later. For now I had bigger demons to de-fang. Namely, myself. Looking at myself in the mirror, I growled, "I'm human now." I didn't know who I was speaking to—Deirdre, myself, whoever was left in the universe to listen. "I will not be taken back to who I was. Not now. Not ever."

Deirdre stepped forward and clasped me with two strong hands. It was a changeling show of solidarity—a clasp meant to be strong and unbreakable. In other words, she meant to hold me tight to let me know that she was on my side ... but I pulled away as if she were a toddler trying to grab my legs.

Even at my most vampiric I couldn't have so easily pulled away from a changeling who meant to hold me. My strength wasn't just back ... I was stronger than ever.

"Milady," Deirdre said, her voice quavering in near helplessness.

I smiled. When the changeling saw my fangs, she growled. I retracted them, making my smile more human. "Find Egya and tell him what's happened to me. Tell him that everything will go ahead as planned. That we only need to break the curse and I'll be human again."

Of course, in my vampire-y selfishness, I didn't add: "And we'll save everyone else in the process."

↔

Popping my fangs back in, I went to my room to dress for tonight's festivities. It was strange, but only hours ago I'd dreaded tonight. Now I relished the hunt. I would smash my fist through Wizard Crusader's helmet, imprinting its metal into his brain. I would—

"Do no such thing," I said out loud. "I am human. HUMAN. Humans do not kill unless absolutely necessary."

Quite the contrary, said the evil voice of the demon within. *Humans kill all the time and their reasons are so petty that to say they are anything but evil is a lie.*

When I was a lonely vampire living in my castle on the highlands of Scotland, I used to listen to that demonic voice—my voice—and relish its words. It was the only company I had … and even though it was me, it wasn't, for so much of what it conjured in my mind were thoughts *I* would never have.

It was like being schizophrenic or suffering from multiple personality disorder. Two voices, both mine, but one was just a bit more *me* than the other.

"Shut up," I said. "I will not kill unless it is to save another life."

Like your own. You are hungry, are you not? And blood—that is what sustains you. That is what will make you whole, give you life. Without it you will perish, so do as you say. Save a life by taking a life. Save yourself.

"Ahh," I said frantically, pulling an outfit together. I put on a Mango v-neck sweater, and as I considered my North Face goose-down jacket, my hand stopped. That monstrosity of fabric was something I had needed to stay warm … as a human.

But cold was something that affected my fragile body. I was no longer fragile. I was no longer so susceptible to such weaknesses.

135

So instead I put on a Barbour Summer Liddesdale quilted jacket, more to complete the outfit than anything, and left my dorm room to battle evil with an evil of my very own.

2 5
A SONG, A PARTY AND A BITE

*J*ustin came through. *More than came through,* I thought as I
walked into the abandoned theater across from Mama's
Diner. The seats had been stripped from the old cinema,
leaving behind a giant cavity where hundreds of people could party.

Abandoned and mostly unused, the old cinema was one of the only
large spaces you could book at a moment's notice. Seemed its owner
had tried to sell the monstrosity several times, but this place must
have had a curse of its own: no one wanted to buy it. So he took whatever little rental fees he could get when someone wanted to book the
place for an event or a party.

And since partying was exactly what we were trying to do, this was
perfect.

Justin sensed my approval. "Not bad, eh? See, here's me being
useful to the team."

"Very," I said, pulling him down for a kiss. Our lips locked and,
forgetting my newly regained old strength, I got a bit too enthusiastic
as I pulled him close.

Too enthusiastic—and fangy. My canine teeth popped out, cutting
his lip and releasing the sweetest nectar known to mortals and gods
alike: blood. Warm, fresh blood from a healthy human.

I think I would have drained him right there if he hadn't pulled away. He touched his lip. "Oww ... I didn't think we were into that."

I want to eat you, I thought.

"After," he said with a wink. Guess I thought that out loud. "First I've got some more setting up to do, and you said something about Cassy singing."

As if the mere mention of her name summoned her, the cinema front doors opened up and Cassy walked in. "Speak of the devil," Justin said.

"Never speak of the devil," she said in an ominous tone, "lest he leave his apartment in Paradise Lot and come knocking on your door."

Justin gulped. "Ahh, so he's real."

"Very," Cassy said. "But from what I hear, his kingdom is a one-bedroom apartment on a wretched island one public funding disaster from becoming a slum."

"Got it," he said. They stared at each other awkwardly before Justin jogged over to a folding table near the wall. He pointed at a boombox, lifting a wireless mic. "Kat said something about you needing to sing a song. This was all I could get on such short notice, but maybe—"

"Thank you, but I don't need such augmentations for my song to be heard."

"You don't?" I asked. "More magic?"

"No, just the essence of who I am." She narrowed her eyes as she looked at me. "Speaking of essence, something is different about you." She leaned in close to get a better sense of me, and then she did something I didn't think sirens, muses or humans did. She touched my eye.

It happened so quickly and so unexpectedly that, even as a vampire with supernatural speed and reflexes, I had no time to react.

Instead I recoiled, a hand over the eye she'd touched. "What did you do that for?" I groaned, then muttered to myself, "I hope your hands are clean ..."

She ignored me, touching her own eye with the finger that had invaded mine. As soon as her fingertip touched her eye, she looked at me and said, "You are—"

Justin was making his way back to us, so I pulled Cassy into the corner. In a harsh whisper, I said, "I'm fine … I mean, I will be fine as soon as we finish this and your little curse is broken." Drawing in a deep breath, I added, "Seems your curse doesn't just make them superheroes. It also does this." I opened my mouth and pointed to my fangy canines.

Her eyes flicked down to my extra-pointy teeth. "Is that what you were?"

I nodded.

"It makes sense that you would seek old powers to help you this day. Also, the mere fact that my curse has touched you means—"

But before she could say anything, Justin tripped over his own feet and fell with a yelp, drowning out Cassy's words.

"Tell me," I said, "stopping this wizard crusader guy … that's not going to lift the curse, is it?"

She shook her head.

"So there's a greater danger lurking in the background?"

Cassy didn't say anything.

"OK," I said, "I get it. I hate this, mind you, but I get it."

I had just turned to see if Justin was OK when she grabbed my arm. There were more tears in her eyes. "I am sorry. I was trying to help and in doing so, I caused so much pain. I am sorry for what I did to them. But I am especially sorry for what I have done to you." She looked down at me with pity in her eyes.

I don't know if it was my vampiric temperament or if it was just unsettling being looked at by someone such as her, but I didn't like it. I pulled my arm away. "Don't worry about it. The curse will be broken and I'll be me again. Let's focus on that."

Cassy drew in a deep breath and nodded. "Yes, what is done is done. Let us focus on what we have control over while we still have that control."

↔

. . .

Cassy wasn't kidding when she said she had a song. I honestly could not tell you if she sang acapella or if a full orchestra accompanied her, if there were lyrics or just music, or if she even opened her mouth.

All those details were lost in the beauty of music unlike anything I had heard before. Cassy may have been a human, but she was touched by a siren and a muse—two powerful creatures made from beauty itself.

And that touch was a part of Cassy in ways that made me shiver with awe.

As the final note of her song left her lips, she closed her eyes and said, "There. Now they will come. And so will he."

PART IV
INTERMISSION

There are so many phonies. So many people who just love hearing the sound of their own voice as they blab their way through life. Good for nothing phonies whose only accomplishment in life will be that they took up way too much space.

But every now and then you meet someone you think is special. Someone who is supposed to break the mold and do something meaningful.

If not meaningful, then at least different.

Or at least try to be different.

But even those guys are phonies. Liars who pretend they care and say they want to make a difference, but when they actually have to do something—anything—they don't. They claim that they are tired or busy or lie by saying something like: "I tried and it didn't work out."

Phonies. I hate them. I hate them all.

But the thing I hate the most about phonies is that, try as you might to get them to see the errors of their ways—their self-deceptions and self-justifications—they don't.

They just walk through life with blinders on, pretending everything's peachy. Well, it's not. It's so far from being good that it drives me crazy.

They'll never see reason.

But that's OK. They will still be useful, for if they can't see reason, perhaps their lives can serve as an example for others to see reason.

For others to take action.

I just have to get others to see the errors of the phonies' ways.

But how can I do that?

It won't be easy, but I know exactly how to cut through the noise and get their attention.

With a bullet and a bang.

26

A SUPERHERO BALL WHOSE
GUEST OF HONOR IS A VILLAIN

As soon as Cassy stopped singing and the awe of her voice wore off enough for us to speak, Justin muttered, "Ahh, that is an ... an amazing way to invite people to a party. I just sent out flyers."

Cassy chuckled, her white cheeks turning a few shades of rose. "Thank you," she said with surprisingly sincere humility, given she must have known how incredible she was.

I could have marveled at Cassy all day, but there was still a lot that needed doing. "OK," I said, shaking my head, "when are your peeps coming?"

I had to nudge Justin with my elbow to get him to respond. "How long, Justin?" I asked again.

"Oh, ahh, let's see." He looked at his watch. "The flyer said 7pm. It's 9pm now, so I'd say any minute."

"Good. Who's manning the door?"

"A couple of my buddies from O^3."

"Another good. OK, you two know what you have to do."

"Yeah, we do," Justin said, then extending his hand to Cassy, he bowed and said, "Milady."

Cassy gave him a wry smile before taking his hand and disappearing. I felt a teeny, tiny pang of jealousy (just a pinch, really) and muttered to the air, "Just remember who butters your toast, buddy. Whatever that means."

Holy guacamole, the Old Librarian in my dream was right: I really wasn't very witty.

With them gone and presumably in place, I got ready as well. My job was simple enough.

I would be the bait.

↔

I got into position as superheroes of all types started walking in the door. You had your usual variety from the Marvel and D.C. universes: Superman, Batman, Spiderman, Hulk, She-Hulk, Scarlet Witch ... and just about any other spandex-clad hero you could name.

You also had He-Man, She-Ra, G.I. Joes, Street Fighters and one enterprising young man dressed in an assortment of cardboard boxes that made him look like Optimus Prime. Fairly typical stuff. Then seven ninjas with what looked like plastic swords entered, and had they been dwarves I would have had a Snow White joke somewhere. But alas, from the way they moved under their black outfits, they were clearly human.

It was when people started entering dressed like Mangi from *Blade of the Immortal* or Rick Hunter from *Robotech* that I started to think: *My kind of party.* I might have enjoyed this night if I wasn't on duty.

Perhaps a hundred dressed-up kids entered and not one of them was an actual superhero. Barring the elderly heroes, I had expected to see the Green Guy, Rhino Boy and the Jessica Jones girl at least, but not one of them showed up, which meant our plan was working.

"Excellent," I muttered to myself, still crouched in position. "So far, so good."

Then Andrew Garner entered in a long trench coat, his blond hair caught in its collar. Typical that he would be the one guy not dressed like a hero. But then again, given his black fingernails, dog collar and leather jacket, he kind of looked like a blond Neo from *The Matrix*—if Neo wasn't trying.

Seeing Andrew was disconcerting. Not because I felt guilty or angry at him, but because I felt nothing one way or another. If anything, I just felt hungry looking at the tall goth. This was the vampire in me acting up ... the apathy of the beast to anything but its own needs. And I knew that if I didn't break the curse soon and become human again, it would be harder and harder to fend off my old ways.

This plan had better work.

Another thirty minutes passed as more and more kids dressed as heroes entered the once-upon-a-time cinema, and still no Wizard Crusader.

Given he was one of Cassy's cursed, he must have heard her song. And since there was no way for him to know how many heroes there were and who was who, the confusion of the situation should have drawn him out.

But Wizard Crusader was, so far, a no-show. I was just about to give up hope when a thought occurred to me. He had stolen the powers of so many heroes, there was no telling what he could do. Also, he might have ditched his old outfit for something less ... geeky.

Batman was cool. A guy dressed in a knight's uniform wasn't.

He could be here, waiting for us to do something ...

OK, I thought, *since I'm supposed to be the bait ...*

I stepped out from the shadows dressed in my own superhero outfit ... a kilt with my family tartan, a black turtleneck, my cherub mask and dirk.

Grabbing the mic, I said, "Welcome, welcome!" The mic screeched in my hand, which made everyone jump. At least I had their attention.

"As I was saying: Welcome."

There was some clapping and cheering.

"As I'm sure everyone is aware, the campus is closed because of a—

how shall I phrase this?—a superhero fight. Forget snow days—we're having a superhero day."

I chuckled at my own joke. No one else did. OK, time to retire that one.

I cleared my throat. "But on a more serious note, the superhero fight did some major damage to the campus, so we'll probably be closed for a while. And since none of us have any classes tomorrow, we thought we'd throw this party!"

The crowd cheered.

"So one last thing before we turn on the music again. I think there is one among you that wasn't invited. A certain LARPing reject with an inflated ego. Let me ask you this, Wizard Crusader, what mask are you wearing now? I know you're probably a sniveling little geek who was never invited to a party before you had superpowers, and you're still a sniveling—"

The mic cut as three kids dressed like ninjas jumped on stage. They pulled out their katanas, which, upon closer examination looked very, very real. One of them grabbed the mic out of my hand and tossed it to a fourth ninja on the dance floor.

"Testing, testing," he said. "Ahh, Master—just as you predicted, she's here."

In a flash, the front door burst open and in walked Wizard Crusader.

Oh, so that wasn't something we had taken into consideration ... Wizard Crusader had minions.

27
NINJA MINIONS AND DARTING VILLAINS

*M*inions. *I should have known. Every villain has a couple and it seems Wizard Crusader has a dozen. Great. But where could someone like him enlist recruits for a mini-army? As someone who has had minions herself, I can guess.*

Anywhere.

All you need to do is walk into a place where a group of like-minded individuals have gathered around a common fear or ideal, display your power, promise you'll help them achieve their goals, and presto! A mini-army at your disposal.

The more vile their goals, the more gruesome the promise, the easier it is to recruit them. A couple fireballs and they'd be sold—

Wizard Crusader laughed. "I also flew around a bit. Oh, and I dropped their last leader off in the Laurentians. Naked. It'll take him three days to get home, and during that whole trip he'll be thinking about how I'm the boss now."

"And your promise?"

The lead ninja took off his hood, revealing a shaved head covered in tattoos of religious symbols. The Christian cross, the Muslim crescent, the Daoist bagua and taijitu, the Hindu *Aum* and the Zoroastrian Faravahar. A HuMan ... I had heard about this new gang rising up in the cities where Others lived. They were dedicated to the eradication of Others. Think Neo-Nazis, except their hate wasn't aimed at immigrants or Jews, but rather the new refugee class comprised entirely of Others.

And because there was no international organization aimed at protecting Other rights yet, the group had yet to be summarily condemned. Humans and their need to officially condemn someone or something. Despite being one now (well, with the exception of my sudden vampiric transformation), I'd never understand this part of being human.

Two HuMan ninjas grabbed my arms, and the other ninjas used swords and threats to keep the party-goers still.

"Shall we?" Wizard Crusader said, taking off his armor but leaving his helmet on. Then putting his feet together, he stretched out his arms like some sadistic Jesus.

Little tentacles of flesh poured out of his arms, stretching away from him and toward every kid dressed as a superhero. There were too many to count and these strange, algae-like growths touched everyone but the ninjas and myself.

I guessed he was going big now—planning to steal everyone's powers. And since he didn't know who had powers and who didn't (save myself and his minions), he was going to tap into every person there.

"You know," I said, as his growths whisked through the air toward their targets, "I get what you're doing. Stealing all their powers and becoming a supreme being yourself. Ever heard of Icarus? The guy who flew too close to the sun?"

Wizard Crusader, who was concentrating on making sure his tentacles flew true, broke his concentration long enough to nod.

"So the legend is, the closer he got to the sun, the more the wax he used to bind his wings started to melt. Well, you know the story … it eventually melted and he crashed to the ground. But that's not what really happened. I know, because a cyclops buddy of mine was actually there when Icarus fell and he told me the story.

"The truth was, he didn't make his wings out of feathers and wax, and the sun didn't melt anything. But he did have wings ... wings he tortured a poor valkyrie into crafting for him. And he used those wings he hadn't made or earned—but rather stole—to fly. For a while he flew quite well. But only for a while. Then air current and wings and resistance and just about every other principle of physics came crashing down on him and he lost control and flew into a cliff face at such an incredible speed that there are probably bits of him still there."

I watched as his tentacles grew, waiting. The first of them were almost on the closest kids.

"He crashed, and why? Because power that is unearned—and worse, unpracticed—is also ineffective." I waited until his little suckers were about to attach ... and the split second before, I cried out, "Now!"

Appearing out of seemingly nowhere, a dozen heroes formed a circle around Wizard Crusader. At the center were my invisible boyfriend and Cassy. Wizard Crusader barely had a second to say, "Holy mythology, Batman!" before Rhino charged, hitting him hard in the chest.

A girl who must have been made out of elastic flattened herself so she looked like a net and bounced Wizard Crusader back against Rhino. As Wizard Crusader rocked back and forth between those two, his helmet fell off to reveal one very scared ... oh shit ... Harold Cheer?

I didn't have time to register who the villain was because a kid in a monk's outfit with an arrow tattooed on his head started doing something that looked like a martial arts kata. A hand made of rock came out of the ground and clasped itself around Wizard Crusader.

And while all that was going on, I vamped out. Well, not blood-drinking vamped out, but using my familiar strength and speed, I grabbed the two ninjas that had been holding me back and threw their racist ... ahh, I mean *Otherist* asses into their fellow misguided friends. Six of them tumbled down and I jumped off the stage.

I grabbed two more and said, "The name's Cherub and I'm crazy." I made sure I had the other ninjas' attention before I added my final, harrowing blow. Summoning the vampire's roar—which sounds like a lion growling through an elephant charge—I cried out, "Run!"

The thing about the vampire's roar: it's savage. Not only did the ninjas run ... so did practically everyone else who wasn't a superhero.

↔

"Harold Cheer," I said. "How are you doing?"

"Not bad, Ka—"

With speed he didn't know I had, I covered his mouth and whispered, "Tut, tut, tut. There are rules to this. I only get to say your name because your mask fell off. Mine is still very much on. Break the rules and I break you. Got it?"

Despite all his powers, Harold was caught and he knew it. He nodded and as he did, the mesh chainmail acting as his helmet's wig cap shook free and fell off. It was then I noticed an earpiece typically used by security operations to stay in touch.

"What's this?" I asked, pulling it off. Putting the earpiece in, I said, "Mayday, mayday—Captain Wizard Crusader is down. I repeat, Captain Wizard Crusader is down." I waited a few seconds for a response and got nothing. "Seems your minion doesn't want to chat."

He smirked at this. "Not a surprise," he said, "since you scared all my minions off. But the guy at the other end of the receiver is not my minion, Cherub." If a word could be poisonous, the way he said *Cherub* was absolutely toxic. "And he knows all about you."

"Really?" I said, lifting an alluring, curious eyebrow—not that anyone saw, since my mask hid all my cuteness away.

And Harold didn't care either way; he wasn't even looking at me. Instead, he scanned the surrounding superheroes and Cassy one by one, as if shooting them with his eyes.

I turned around to see all the heroes standing in a circle looking at Harold. Most of them didn't know who this dweeb was, but I could tell a couple did. Their surprise shone with particular brightness as they realized the kid they had dismissed as harmless was actually the most violent of the bunch.

They were surprisingly restrained, partly because while they were invisible, Cassy and Justin had told them as much as they could about what was going on. But their restraint wasn't just because they heard Cassy and believed her. We were off campus, so they weren't being compelled by the conditions of the curse to act in one way or another. And uncompelled, these superheroes revealed themselves for who they truly were … kids who were scared and no more interested in having superpowers than a monkey desires to go to outer space.

"You know, my whole life I've been made fun of for being smaller, weaker, more passionate," Harold said, shaking his head. "Also for being smart, and none of their mockery ever bothered me."

Since he didn't know most of these kids, I assumed he meant the royal *their*.

"The only thing that ever really got me mad," Harold continued, "was when they made fun of me for playing *Dungeons and Dragons*. 'Ohh, Harold the Wizard,' they'd say. 'Where's your dragon?' 'Done playing in the dungeon?' But in all their taunts and mockery, they never got two things: One, *Dungeons and Dragons* is a complex game that, despite its name, really doesn't have that many dragons in it. And two, the spells in that game were absolutely *inspiring*."

As he uttered the word "inspiring," his eyes glowed yellow. Three giant, disembodied hands appeared behind the kid dressed as a monk, Rhino and—gulp—Justin.

28

INVISIBLE HANDS ARE THE DEVIL'S PLAYTHINGS

The hands grabbed each of the heroes and the three kids started aging immediately. This wasn't my first battle with a wizard, so I did what worked in the past with those blowhards: I punched Harold. Square in the nose. I was trying to break his spell and wound up breaking his nose as well. *Bonus points: me.*

His head rocked back, but looking over my shoulder, I saw that his spell held. This might not have been my first fight with a wizard, but it was my first fight with a wizard imbued with the powers of a half-dozen superheroes.

I punched him again, this time not holding back any of my vampiric strength. My fist connected with a sonic boom and I justified the very real possibility that my punch could kill him with thoughts of saving Justin.

His head snapped back and for a second I thought I had punched it clean off.

But he lifted it again, smiling as the blood from his nose ran down to his lips and painted his teeth crimson. I had just drawn my fist back for a third strike when Harold said, "Uh, uh, uh. Two is all I need."

"For what—?" I started, but when I saw the purple currents running through him I knew what he was about to do.

How could I have been so stupid? was my last thought before Harold unleashed the kinetic energy I'd put in him with those punches. Using the power he had stolen from Justin, he sent pieces of the stone hand that had been holding him in every direction.

I was thrown across the room, but because of my vampiric agility —and staying true to my name—I managed to land on my feet.

Harold, freed, used Rhino's power to charge, though not at me or any of the other heroes, but rather the back stage and brick wall behind him.

I chased after him, only sparing a second to watch my once young boyfriend curl over with arthritis and the pockmarks of age.

↔

Harold might have had superpowers and the ability to fly, but I was a vampire, which meant that not only was I fast, but I was also an incredible climber.

Outside, Harold took to the air, but from the awkward way he lifted off the ground I could tell he was hurt. No, more than hurt— he was using Underdawg's flight ability, not Comet Boy's, and the only reason I could think of for him to be doing that was because Underdawg's powers came with the pain-numbing effects of marijuana.

I guess my punches got to him after all.

Jumping onto the wall of the adjacent building, I scampered up until I was on its rooftop. Then charging forward with agility and speed that would make any parkour enthusiast positively die with envy, I managed to latch onto Harold's leg before I got onto his back and rode him like an angry Swedish masseuse with a chip on her shoulder.

He tried to buck me off, but I dug my nails into his plate and mail armor. He'd need to strip naked to get me off, and even then, I was determined to latch onto whatever dangling appendages he had under all this armor.

Bucking, dipping up and down, he flailed mid-air, and I used his distraction and panic to steer his flight toward Montreal's mountain ... and more specifically, right over Mont Royal's Cemetery. Once we were headed in the right direction, I bent over and whispered into Harold's ear, "You're going to have to go much faster than this to rid yourself of me."

Then I unleashed my inner demon and bit down hard on Harold's neck.

↔

In Islam, comets, meteors and shooting stars are not space rocks entering our atmosphere and burning up on entry—they are angels being kicked out of the Emerald City of Qa, the home of jinn.

Whereas I believe most streaks in the night sky are probably debris entering our atmosphere, not all of them are. Some are indeed angels getting the boot from one of God's heavenly bouncers.

And the thing about getting the boot: your punishment doesn't just stop at *entry denied*. That would be too easy and thus, God and his smokeless jinn created Earth-bound beings that would wait below to continue the torturous festivities.

Ghouls.

They were to jinn what orcs were to elves. In other words, the jinn's ugly cousins. But unlike orcs, who were simply agents of chaos, ghouls were the second part of the *kick 'em out, punish 'em below* cycle.

How did they do that? Well, it started with the ghouls capturing these poor, hapless falling angels and then imprisoning them until they got a sign from up above that their captives were to be set free.

And it just so happened that there was a comet-catching family of ghouls below who owed me a favor.

Giant grappling hooks shot to the sky and embedded themselves into Harold's armor and flesh, and with a mighty yank, they pulled his golden, glowing ass down to Earth.

Harold fought against their hooks, and in his enormous efforts to break free managed to dislodge me. I came tumbling down to Earth ahead of him, and this time there was no one to leap up and save me.

Vampires can die. I know—I've killed a couple myself. It takes a lot and you really have to come after them, but if you're able to deliver enough damage to their bodies, they will cease to be.

As I fell, I didn't know if a fall from this height was enough to kill me. *I guess I'll just have to wait and see*, I thought as I fell.

And as the earth drew closer, I thought that dying this way wouldn't be so bad. I would have died trying. And what's more, I would have died trying even though I was a vampire now. I was both proud and saddened by this thought.

Proud because I had fought the demon within so that I could do the right thing.

Saddened because now that I knew the beast could be tamed, I wished I had tried to many centuries ago.

Oh well, I thought in that last second, *no point in crying over spilt blood now.*

↔

I hit the ground with a muted splat.

And the first indication that I hadn't died was seeing Deirdre and Egya sitting by my side as I came to. My head rang so loudly I couldn't hear what they were saying, but the worried looks in their eyes told me everything I needed to know. They cared. Deirdre cried, which was to be expected; as powerful as the changeling was, one of her most endearing qualities was that she always expressed her emotions … good, bad or confused.

What was unexpected were Egya's tears. During the months I had gotten to know the Ghanaian, he had never expressed any emotions besides anger and laughter. This … this was new.

I tried to sit up, meaning to walk it off, but neither of them would let me stand. So I lay there as my body rapidly repaired itself. And it was fast, faster than it had ever been in the past for lesser injuries.

"Girl," Egya said, "you got something in your teeth." I barely heard him through my ringing ears, but the gesture that went along with his words was enough for me to touch my lips.

Blood.

More specifically, Harold's blood. Things started to click. Drinking blood didn't give you your victim's powers and abilities (if it did, I would have had a real taste for angels), but it does give you their resilience, and the combination of Justin and Rhino's resilience was probably what saved me.

"The ghouls—" I started, but Egya hushed me.

"They got the crusader fellow in one of their tombs. They'll hold him until he is human. They said they owe the angel who cannot fly for saving them from the dog who could."

"Good," I said, laying back down and letting my body do what it must.

↔

I must have lain there for an hour or so before I was whole enough to get up. The ringing had subsided and, after refusing Deirdre's offer to carry me for the dozenth time, I started down the hill back toward the cinema. Deirdre and Egya tried to come with me, but I insisted they stay. I couldn't risk Harold escaping.

I needed Wizard Crusader detained because the real doom was yet to happen. And Cassandra couldn't warn us … so I needed everything to be as uncomplicated as possible.

They resisted, but ultimately agreed.

That done, I walked down the hill. I needed to figure out what that "doom" was, but more importantly, I needed to get back to Cassy and her superheroes.

LEAD FOR YOUR HEART, PENNIES FOR YOUR EYES

*R*eturning to the theater, I saw the superheroes milling about. The group (what do you call a group of super-heroes? Assemble? Power?) of superheroes had splintered into small groups, speaking in hushed whispers among themselves. There were no normals around. I guessed the sight of Harold and his tentacles was enough to send all of them packing.

Cassy was walking among them, comforting them as best she could, and also telling them as much as her curse allowed.

I approached the Prophetess of Doom. "Harold has been taken care of ... he won't bother us again tonight." She nodded, breathing a sigh of relief that I've seen on aid workers in war zones. It was the relief that came from one less thing to deal with. Sure, that doesn't make all the chaos go away, or even make life particularly better or easier, but it was still one less thing. "So, I guess all we have to do—"

My words were cut off when I saw a very old man sitting on the stage, being propped up by several cushions gathered from the Gone-Gods know where. He was bald, liver spots replacing what had once been a skull filled with lush black hair. His blue eyes were replaced by a depressed gray-blue, and his once flawless skin that had hung tight on his cheeks now looked like a cotton shirt left too long in the washing machine.

Justin. And he looked old.

Older than what I should look like.

I walked over to him and took his frail hand in mine. I had been around enough humans at their different stages of life to know he didn't have long on this Earth. Even if the curse was broken, he wouldn't revert back to his nineteen-year-old self.

He wouldn't revert because Cassandra's curse had nothing to do with aging. That effect had been part of Harold's powers.

Justin was old and would remain old for the rest of his days … as few as they were.

He was going to die. Maybe not right now, but I was sure he wouldn't see the New Year's bells ring and there was nothing I could do about it.

No—that wasn't entirely true, was it? I was a vampire now. I could bite him, sire him, rip away his soul and infect him with a demon that would allow him to live forever. I could …

The demon might have been inside me. It might have stripped away my own soul, slowly turning me into an uncaring, hateful person. But I wasn't lost to it yet. I still had much of what made me, *me*.

And I would hold onto that for as long as I could.

That meant no spreading my vampiric disease no matter the circumstances. That meant no turning Justin no matter how much I wanted to.

"Hey," he said, his voice as foreign to him as it was to me. "How are you?"

"I had a tumble, but other than that I'm fine."

"I can see that," he said, picking a blade of grass off my sweater. "You must have really fallen a long way to get through all the snow and stuff."

"Yeah, you could say that …" I went silent, not sure what else to say.

"Cherub," he whispered, "I don't suppose you'd help an old man backstage? I need to talk to you and my knees aren't what they once were."

↔

I helped Justin backstage where we could speak in private. Even though we only walked a dozen or so yards, he was out of breath and propping himself up on a table that stood on the stage. "So …" he said.

Despite his aged voice, I recognized the tone. He was going to say something funny. But what could be funny now? "You know how they say, look at your lover's parents to see what you're going to get when they're older?" He made a *ta-da* gesture. "Well, what do you think?"

I gave him an appraising look. "Not bad. Not bad at all."

"You know, I always thought if I was really lucky I'd get to grow old with you. Of course, when I thought that I kind of guessed you'd be old, too …" He trailed off as he smiled. Even old, his smile was beautiful.

I forced a chuckle as the irony hit my brain like a barbwire-covered bat. He was old and I wouldn't age a day. How fair was that?

Justin's face went serious. "I'm guessing I'm ninety. Maybe more. I didn't have much time to prepare this given I generally don't have much time at all, but …" He groaned as he shimmied off the chair. I helped as best I could, but he pushed me away. "No, I need to do this on my own."

He lowered himself onto one aged knee. "My friend, my lover, my superhero … you are the best thing that has happened to me and if you will only say one simple word, I can die happy." He pulled out a ring from his shirt pocket and presented it to me.

I felt tears roll down my still youthful cheeks as the word he longed to hear tried to find its way out of my mournful throat and into the world.

But before I could utter that one simple word, I heard a yell.

. . .

↔

"We'll get back to this," I said, putting my mask back on. "Stay right there and ... we'll get back to this. Promise!"

I ran back to the auditorium, only pausing to look back to see one very old, very disappointed Justin.

Shit, I'm such an asshole, I thought as I propelled myself into a room full of superheroes.

In the middle I saw Cassy crying as she tried to scream something that no one could hear.

We couldn't hear it because overhead lights kept falling, the sprinkler system had gone off, the theater floor cracked in with a loud thud ... as every possible and impossible catastrophe happened in that room all at once and all with the single purpose of preventing us from hearing what she had to say.

But from the way she wailed I could tell she was screaming one word over and over again. One single word that meant the difference between life and death ... one word that the gods thought would be funny if no one could hear.

Screw that, I thought. *The gods are gone and so are their crap rules.*

Using my vampiric strength and speed, I leapt from the stage, landing right next to her. She looked down at me, her eyes filled with dread and panic as she screamed that word again. As the word tumbled out of her lips, the theater screen ripped with a loud *zzzzippp*, drowning her word again.

She started to point, but as she raised her hand, a friggin' piece of ceiling plaster fell on her arm, forcing it down.

I didn't know what to do and thought about how in the last twenty-four hours I'd had fireballs and fists and super-speed freaks attack me ... and survived. I'd fallen from impossible heights and survived.

And now that I couldn't hear one word, I was probably going to die.

If only the world would stop breaking and the ground she stood on would stop shaking, maybe I could …

How could I be so stupid? I thought. *Her curse, what was it again? Cassandra shall walk this Earth, never to be heard, never to help a single soul, never to die.*

Curses are cryptic, but they are also specific. And it is in the small print that you can break a curse.

I somersaulted toward Cassandra and tucking in low, I placed her in a fireman's hold as I leapt forward and as high up as I could.

Thank the GoneGods for vampiric strength, because we managed to latch onto the velvet walls lining the old cinema auditorium. And it was there, with Cassandra's feet dangling ten feet above the ground, that I heard her.

"Run!" she cried.

"Run," I repeated.

Cassandra's eyes widened in disbelief. "You can hear me?"

"Yes. Run. Where?" I said, conscious that time was of the essence (yuck, what a cliché, but clichés are clichés for a reason).

"Run out the back. He's almost here. Run!"

I dropped down with Cassy in my arms and yelled, "Everyone— out the back! Now. Those who can help the old ones, do so right away."

The superheroes hesitated and I screamed using my vampiric roar, "NOW!"

The superheroes didn't need to be told a third time. They all rushed out the back, the two superfast kids grabbing Rhino Boy and the monk as one of the unaged superheroes helped Justin.

In a flash the heroes were gone and with their disappearance, the room went silent.

Only Cassy and I remained, our ears adjusting to the absence of sound.

And it was in that absence we both heard the click of a gun.

30

CLICK, CLACK, BANG, LIKE IT
AIN'T NO THANG ...

Except It Is a Thing—a Very Big Thing, Indeed

I knew that click. I'd heard it before, during a brief stint I
spent in Okinawa. During the war. I was there because I'd
figured war meant lots of dying humans, which meant easy hunting
grounds. I wasn't wrong. What I hadn't taken into account, though,
was the advancement of human guns and how much more destruction they were capable of. When I was a young vampire, I only had to
worry about muskets and other flint-based weapons. Hell, even a
cannon in the 1800s did less damage than a machine gun in the 1940s.

Machine guns are probably one of the few things I feared as a
vampire, so I got to know their sounds well. That click belonged to
someone pulling the hammer back on a monstrosity that could spew
out dozens of specially-designed-to-kill bullets per second.

Without hesitation, I grabbed Cassy, hugging her as dozens of
steel-tipped bullets ripped into my back.

They tore me apart with such ferocity I feared they would fly
through me and into her. I suspected if I wasn't a vampire with hard-

ened skin and tougher-than-normal internal organs and bones, they would have. The destructive power of that machine was incredible.

Within seconds that felt like an eternity, the clip emptied and the gunman needed to reload.

That was our chance and, as hurt as I was, I pushed Cassy to run.

She hesitated, but I didn't give her a choice. "Now it's my turn, so hear me and hear me well ... run."

"But he'll kill you," she said.

"He'll try," I replied, extending my fangs under my mask. "Now run!"

And Cassandra, Prophetess of Doom cursed never to be heard, did exactly that. She ran.

↔

With Cassy gone, I allowed the pain of the bullets to hit me. I fell to my knees, panting. It was difficult to kill a vampire, no doubt about it, but do enough damage to our body and we're dead. That was the other thing about Cassy's curse ... she only saw visions of what was going to happen, but not necessarily how they happened. She had no idea that gathering the kids here was probably the worse thing we could have done. Like shooting fish in a barrel ... or rather, super-heroes in a theatre. If I hadn't been able to break the curse and hear her, they would all be dead. And given how bullet-ridden my body was, so would I. But I heard her in time to warn them. They got away. For now.

But I knew that was only a temporary solution. Prophesies, especially the vague, devoid of details ones, tended to find a way to come true. And everything Cassy and I did ... the superheroes, stopping the Crusader, this party ... they were all steps that delayed the fruition of the prophesy, but did little to actually stop this killer from showing up with his tools of destruction.

We only delayed him. But he would keep coming until he found a way to kill those kids. He was the mystical version of the Terminator and unless I stopped him right here and right now, he would keep coming after them until the prophesy was fulfilled.

I doubted I could survive another clip unloaded in me. But I was also too weak to do anything but talk. My body needed time to heal and as heavy footsteps approached, I feared that I wouldn't get the time I needed.

"Cherub girl," I heard a familiar voice say. "I thought you were one of the good guys."

"I am," I said, the effort causing me to spit out blood. Internal bleeding. That sucks, too.

Another click as the machine gun's hammer cocked. "It's amazing you're still standing after all that."

"And yet here I am."

"So you're an Other, huh? Should have figured. It's a shame to kill you, but ..."

"Hold on," I said. "Before you do it, can I at least see your face?"

"Interesting. Is this some kind of noble death, need-to-see-the-face-of-your-killer kind of thing?"

"Not really. It's more of a I-want-to-see-who-I'll-be-waiting-to-meet-in-hell-so-I-can-kill-them-there kind of thing."

"There is no hell. Not anymore."

"Fair enough. But still. Grant me this one wish."

There was a hesitation, then heavy steps walked in front me and I saw a tall man with a bandana over his face. He was wearing a black hoodie, making his face unrecognizable, but I still knew who he was. "Andrew," I said. "Didn't think you were the trigger-happy type."

He paused, turning his head to one side in confusion. "What gave me away?"

"Your fingernails."

He lifted a gloved hand that covered only four fingers. He had cut the trigger finger off his glove. "Observant."

"So I've been told."

He chuckled. Using his exposed finger, he lowered his own mask. "So what do you say, an unmasking for an unmasking?"

"Sure," I said, my body mending but still far from useful. I didn't need seconds to heal—I needed hours. Somehow I doubted I would get that. I lifted my mask up. "Ta-da."

Andrew smiled something wicked. "The gods may be gone, but karma is still in full effect."

"I don't catch your meaning," I said, coughing more blood.

"When you quit the race, you made it to the top of my list. I had thought about hunting you down just to make sure I got you before—you know," he made a gesture as though shooting himself in the head. "But when I saw all these so-called superheroes in one place, all those phonies who pretend to care, but really don't … I realized it was too good an opportunity to pass up."

"So you went home to gear up."

"And gear up I did," he said, lifting the nozzle of his gun to my forehead. "So before you go bye-bye, what kind of Other are you anyway? I mean, you look so human …"

"That's because I am."

"Sure you are."

"I am. At least for now."

He shrugged. "Human or not, doesn't really matter. You're a phony like all the rest of them. A phony who deserves to die—"

There was a thud as a rock hit Andrew on the shoulder. "Ow," he cried out, turning to look up as another rock fell from the upper auditorium. Looking up, I saw a very old Justin and a very angry Cassy hurling rocks from the theater's upper balconies.

Thank the GoneGods for small miracles, I thought a split second before Andrew's machine gun started to roar.

↔

Andrew fired up toward the balcony. Cassy was fast enough, pulling back from the balcony so she couldn't be seen.

Justin wasn't as fast and a bullet ripped through his ninety-year-old shoulder, knocking him over.

Seeing my boyfriend fall gave me the strength to lunge forward, and biting into Andrew's ankle, I said, "No one shoots my boyfriend but me."

Andrew screamed in pain, turning his gun on me. I grabbed the nozzle, pushing it away so the bullets couldn't strike my body. Hot lead flew harmlessly into the ground, sparing my body from further holes.

The only part that hurt was the heat of the muzzle. I could smell burning flesh as he continued pulling the trigger until … *click, click, click* … the sound of an empty gun.

I yanked the machine gun out of his hands and tossed it away, the skin from my palm ripping away from my own hand as I did so. Then I hit his knee—hard. It popped back and he tumbled over.

Face to face, I thought about ripping out his throat and draining him. I would have, too, had it not been for Justin's groans.

Justin, my human boyfriend, also served as an anchor to my own humanity at that moment. So instead of eating him, I punched him in the nose. Hard.

His head snapped back as his eyes rolled to the back of his head and he lost consciousness.

31

HOW MANY LIVES IS YOUR OWN WORTH?

*E*ven the little bit of blood taken from Andrew's ankle was enough to send my body into rapid healing mode, and by the time I made it to the balcony, I had healed enough that I could go another round with any villain stupid enough to get in my way.

Not that I wanted to … I'd much prefer a hot bath and a week of sleep.

I made my way to Justin's side, where Cassy was tending to his wound. I could feel his life force leaving him. It was a flesh wound, but his body was too old to survive the trauma. If he was young, maybe. But as he was, I figured he had minutes left.

Wiping away tears, I said, "You shouldn't have come back. You shouldn't have—"

"And what?" he said in that tone of his. "Let you have all the fun? No way, no how." And despite being in so much obvious pain, he smiled. The smug bastard, I chuckled to myself as I looked him over. His body was shutting down and even though it was only a shoulder wound, he was definitely running out of time.

I thought about biting him again. I could give him the strength to survive this wound. I could give him eternal life.

I would have, too, except when I tried to extend my fangs, nothing happened. They were gone. The superhero curse had been lifted and I was just a normal girl again.

I was normal, which meant there was nothing I could do to save Justin.

Despair had fallen over me when a gentle hand touched mine. I looked up to see Cassy smiling. "You heard me," she said.

"I did," I said. "Not that it did any good."

She shook her head as she loosened the braid that had held back her hair. With silver hair cascading over her, she said, "You heard me and I am free. Finally, I am free."

As she spoke, I felt Justin squeeze my hand. Looking down at him, I saw his liver spots disappear and his wrinkles smooth out. His cataracts cleared up and his arthritic joints regained their virility. He was becoming ... young.

"How?" I muttered as I watched the hand of time turn back for him. Justin was aging backward.

Soon Justin would be his nineteen-year-old self again.

Which meant—

"Cassy, stop," I said, turning to Cassandra. But it was too late for this woman. This sister of Helen, daughter of Priam, this creature who was touched by the siren Ligeia and blessed by the muse Calliope, this former Prophetess of Doom.

She was already old.

Cassandra was burning away her life to give life back to Justin. And from the way she aged, I knew she wasn't just restoring Justin. She was restoring them all.

"Stop," I begged, but Cassandra simply shook her head as she continued burning her life away, using her magic to undo all that she had done.

"You know," she said, "I have lived for over three thousand years never able to save anyone. But you heard me, you broke my curse and for the first time in my long, long life, *I* am the one who gets to play the hero."

↔

Cassandra burnt enough time to return all the aged superheroes back to their rightful ages. She burnt enough time to reverse the damage on the cinema and wipe Harold and Andrew's memory clean of who Cherub really was.

She burnt enough time to heal Justin's wounds.

And when she was done, she stood up, no longer the impossibly gorgeous girl, but rather an elegant, elderly woman with an ever-present, infectious smile.

↔↔↔

During Cassandra's remaining days, Boggie tended to her needs, loving her as any grateful human being loves someone who is more than a grandparent and friend.

Andrew was arrested for possessing firearms and attempted murder. He was given a ridiculously light sentence after what he tried to do. I guess you needed bodies for them to lock you up and throw away the keys.

And for me. I should have been happy, but I wasn't. I was human again, the people I loved were safe ... I should have been happy. But all I felt was an emptiness I couldn't shake.

Maybe I was tired. Or still shaken up from everything that had happened. But then a thought rushed into me that I prayed to whoever would listen wasn't true: *Maybe becoming human for a second time somehow tainted me. Cursed me.*

I pushed away the thought, insisting to myself that I was exhausted. That, and my faith in humanity had been challenged by everything that had happened.

Those were the lies I said to myself. The lies I so desperately wished were true.

32

ALL'S WELL THAT ENDS WELL ... WELL, MAYBE NOT

The following days were a blur of police interviews and depositions. After a couple weeks, it all died down and life returned to normal. Well, as normal as my life could ever be.

I lost the Gardner Hall presidency race ... but Aimee won. Good for her, she might have been the shyest candidate to ever win the seat, but she was a good soul, and with her at the helm, I suspected this year would be less about beer and more about things that mattered.

Speaking of things that mattered—to me, at least: I still had to deal with Justin and his proposal, but I avoided him, unable to bring myself to speak to him. Even though everything had happened over two weeks ago, I was still feeling empty. Lost.

There was a sadness in me I couldn't shake. A depression that had latched onto my very being, digging its claws deeper and deeper into my heart.

I knew I was in real trouble when *Legally Blonde* did nothing to lift my spirits.

There was something wrong with me. And so I did what I always do when faced with a problem I don't understand.

I researched.

In the archives of the Other Studies Library, I looked up every piece of lore about the vampiric virus and its effects on a person. I researched all I could find—which wasn't much—and might have continued to do so had I not heard a crackle coming from my desk.

It sounded like a radio. I opened my top drawer and looked inside, my hand hesitating to reach in as my mind conjured images of some crackling mini-demon waiting to bite my fingers off.

But there was no mini-demon in there. Rather it was something much, much worse. It was Harold's earpiece.

It crackled again.

I put it to my ear. "Hello."

A raspy sigh seeped out of the earpiece's speakers, "Ahh, finally we speak, Katrina Darling."

The voice sounded old. Ancient, even … but it wasn't one I recognized. "I guess we do," I said. "But you have me at a disadvantage. You are?"

"The one that counseled that horrid excuse for a crusader about dealing with you. I had meant to use the boy to break you. With all that power, he should have done so easily. But instead, you broke him."

"Oh, you're talking about Harold?"

"Aye."

"OK, so you tried to kill me—"

"Break you," a rasp interrupted.

"Whatever. Still, you called Harold 'a horrid excuse for a crusader' and I happen to agree with that assessment, so you can't be all that bad."

The raspy voice chuckled, which sounded more like someone with bronchitis trying to dislodge phlegm. Lots of it. "I have been warned that you like to say silly things when frightened, and honest words when you think no one is listening."

"And I have been warned not to talk to strangers. So unless you tell me your name, I guess this is goodbye—"

"How do you feel, Katrina Darling? If I were to hazard a guess, the word 'empty' comes to mind."

Empty. That was exactly how I felt … but how did he know?

"Yes," I finally said, wanting to see what he knew about this cloud that seemed to follow me wherever I went.

"Do you know what happens to a human's soul when they become a vampire?"

My eyes widened. A few months back I had had an unpleasant encounter with my mother that led to me speaking with an ex-vampire and powerful alchemist named Lizile. During our brief and very weird encounter, she read my future, but not before telling me about a powerful magical item called the Rooh Ina'ah—the Soul Jar.

She said I would play a pivotal role in the war that was to come ... and that it had something to do with that Soul Jar.

"I see you do," the raspy voice said, taking my long silence as an affirmation. "Several of our kind have been looking for it—"

"Why? So you can become vampires again?" I threw in as much venom as those words would allow.

"So we can live forever," he said without hesitation. "But alas, the jar is lost to us. What is *not* lost to us is the path that a soul follows when seeking the jar. And your soul, when it left your body the night before you awoke as what you once were—"

"A vampire. Jesus, can't you guys just talk straight? What's with the 'night before you awoke as you once were' crap?"

"Still frightened, I see," he said. "Good, your fear will be an asset when making the most important decision you have before you."

"Which is?" I said, faking a yawn.

"Which is," he said, his voice momentarily losing its rasp, "to find your soul or not. That emptiness within ... it exists because your soul remains trapped."

It took me a second to register what he was saying. My soul trapped, and not within me? How could that be? *He's lying*, I thought. *He must be.* But given the hollow emptiness consuming me, a part of me believed him.

I'd never felt such nothingness before. A nothingness that sprung from my heart and infested every corner of my being. When I was a vampire, the demon filled those parts of me ... but now I was free of the demon, a human again, and all I felt was a hole left by the demon's absence.

A hole that should have been filled by my soul.

"How? How do you know?" I said, not trying to hide my quavering voice.

"You are not the only one whose soul has yet to return."

I closed my eyes and felt a warm tear roll down my cheek. But instead of sadness or despair, I just felt this awful void. I knew I was sad, but at the same time I wasn't. The emptiness was refusing to let my emotions fill it and as this strange, confused conflict raged within me, I said, "You said 'to find my soul or not.' I'm assuming you believe it's in the Soul Jar."

"Aye."

"And yet you haven't found it. Why?"

"Because I already asked my question, Katrina."

I truly wished this was one of those moments when the cryptic villain made no sense and I could go stomping off, ignoring their ridiculous way of speaking. But the sad truth was, I knew exactly what he was talking about: "the Amulet of Souol."

"Indeed. The amulet grants its owner the answer to one question and only one. It must be the question that consumes you, that fills the very hole left by your soul. Do not ask it now. This emptiness, this pain—it is new. You need to wait until the void consumes you to the point of breaking. Then ask."

"And what? You're going to join me on a friendly excursion to wherever this friggin' Soul Jar is?"

"Still afraid. Good. Use that." And before I could say anything else, the earpiece crackled and the man with the raspy voice disappeared.

Shit, I thought, thinking back to my dream with the Old Librarian. So it really was him warning me somehow.

How? I had no idea.

I considered hitting the books, doing research and figuring this out, but I was bone-tired. And what's more, I was fighting to care.

Another time, I thought, walking out of the Other Studies Library.

"Another time," I muttered out loud this time as I turned off the lights.

↔

I walked up the hill, barely thinking, barely conscious of where I was and moving only on autopilot. I made it to my room where a sock was hanging. I briefly considered that Deirdre had a suitor over—*lucky guy or gal, or both*, I thought—and not going in. But then I remembered it was Deirdre ... she was so uninhibited that she'd probably have a full conversation in mid ... ahhh ... stride.

I walked in, but instead of seeing a naked changeling, I saw a fully clothed, newly made young man.

"Justin," I said, forcing myself to smile. "I thought—"

"I had to see you," he said. "And thank you for, you know ... saving me again."

I pointed at his shoulder. "You were still hurt and well, I didn't save you. You know who did."

"I do. And I've thanked her, too. That lady has a gift basket from the Body Shop with enough anti-aging moisturizer to turn her back into an infant."

He giggled at his joke. I did not.

"Look, I know I, you know, proposed and all ... and I'm guessing you avoiding me is your answer, but—"

"Justin, do we have to do this now?"

"Just hear me out. I only proposed because I thought I literally had days to live. And I very selfishly wanted to spend them with you. Now that I'm young again, I'd like to take back my proposal. For now, at least. I might ask again way, way, way down the line."

He got on one knee. "Katrina Darling ... will you not marry me, but instead, can we go back to the way things were?"

He gave me his big, goofy smile that normally made me weak in the knees, but now did little for me.

"You would make me the happiest man on the planet if you would just say, 'Yes.' "

I shrugged and said, "Yes," less ceremonially than the situation required. I was tired. And apparently soulless, too.

He leapt to his feet. "Woohoo! She's not going to marry me. She's not going to marry me!" He tried to grab me to join in his dance, but I pulled away.

His face went somber. "You OK?"

"No," I said, too tired to lie. "I'm exhausted and just can't shake this horrible feeling. Ever since I ... you know." I pointed at where my fangs would be and gestured them going up into my gums.

"You're human again after briefly being a vampire. That's tough. A part of you that you thought would be gone forever came back ... and now that it's gone again, you're kind of sad." He took my hands in his and kissed them both. "And that's OK. You're allowed to feel this way."

"I am?"

"You are. And it might take a wee bit of time to feel better ... and that's OK, too."

"It is?"

"It is."

I shook my head and did something I hadn't done since that night in the theater. I smiled.

I walked over to my bed, only taking the time to take off my jacket before falling in. "Thank you," I said. "And I'm really sorry ... truly I am, but I am so tired."

"Of course, of course," he said, standing by the bed and waiting expectantly.

"I'm tired."

"No hanky panky. I won't even try—I swear." He made a cross sign over his heart.

"Fine," I said, drawing back the covers. Hanky panky ... that was a good one. I would normally have laughed at that one, or at least smiled. But this time I don't think I even reacted.

He jumped into bed with me. "So I guess this is one of those all's-well-that-ends-well scenarios?" Justin said.

" 'All's well that ends well?' " I raised a curious eyebrow.

"Shakespeare," he said. "I know how much you like his work and, well, I've been reading. And I'm trying to score a couple points with you."

"The scoreboard is closed. Too tired to remember. Save it for some time when I wouldn't trade my soul—" I stopped myself from finishing.

"For a good's night sleep," he said, finishing my sentence. "I understand."

He drew in close, seeking to cuddle me, but I was asleep before I could feel the weight of his arms around me.

33

A BRIEF EPILOGUE

That night Justin falls asleep with Kat in his arms. He does not dream of being a superhero, nor does his mind wander toward thoughts of heroism or gallantry. He doesn't even dream of Katrina.

His mind is an empty box filled only with the intangible touch of happiness. But that's the thing about empty boxes: they are made to be filled. And as Justin drifts deeper and deeper into sleep, a growing darkness fills the empty space.

It is a mist … a specter of black that ebbs and flows as it contaminates more and more of this box.

Once this darkness covers the walls with black, it starts to summon other parts within Justin. It begins with his memories: of Katrina Darling and her friends. But it doesn't stop there … the University, Montreal, being a student. The darkness wishes to learn it all.

When the darkness feels it has learned all it needs to know, it leaves the box that is Justin's mind, seeping into another place within Justin to be contained. It does not take long for the darkness to find what it is looking for.

Infecting Justin's beating heart, the darkness enters its chambers, relishing the pulsing rush and push of blood.

"Here," it crackles. "Here is a box worthy of Dybbuk."

ALSO BY RAMY VANCE

Mortality Bites Series

Mortality Bites

Family Matters

Superhero Me!

Orphaned Follies

Dawn of a Thousand Sunsets

Three Dead Gods

Run, Kat, Run

Encantado Dreams

The Heaviest of Burdens

Looking for a great deal? Grab these book bundles...

Setting Fires with Dragons - complete series

Mortality Bound - complete series

GoneGod World - Complete series

Series Starter - Bundle

ALSO BY RAMY VANCE

Mortality Bites Series

Mortality Bites

Family Matters

Superhero Me!

Orphaned Follies

Dawn of a Thousand Sunsets

Three Dead Gods

Run, Kat, Run

Encantado Dreams

The Heaviest of Burdens

Shattered Vows

GoneGod World Series

GoneGod World

Keep Evolving

CrystalDreams

Penemue's Inferno

Looking for a great deal? Grab these book bundles...

Setting Fires with Dragons - complete series

Mortality Bites - complete series

Mortality Bound - Complete series

Series Starter - Bundle